A CAPITAL CALAMITY

Escapades in Doomsdayland

—A Novel

by Fred Kaplan

Library of Congress Cataloging-in-Publication Data

Fred Kaplan, A Capital Calamity, Escapades in Doomsdayland—A Novel

Summary: This is the story of a cynical defense consultant whose mischief plunges the world into a cataclysmic crisis. Now, along with the CIA director (who is also a bitter ex-girlfriend), a former school chum who's now an NSA hacker, a garrulous Wall Street tycoon-turned-secretary of defense, and a beautiful intrepid journalist (who may or may not be flirting with him for a big story), he must stop the war that he helped start.

ISBN: 978-1-939282-54-5

Published by Miniver Press, LLC, McLean Virginia
Copyright 2024 Fred Kaplan

First edition October 2024
This book is set in Bembo Std

Cover by Rachael Adams https://rachaeladams.org

DEDICATION

For Brooke, Maxine, and Sophie,
this time a bit more than usual

OTHER BOOKS BY FRED KAPLAN

The Bomb: Presidents, Generals, and the Secret History of Nuclear War

Dark Territory: The Secret History of Cyber War

The Insurgents: David Petraeus and the Plot to Change the American Way of War

1959: The Year Everything Changed

Daydream Believers

The Wizards of Armageddon

Much of what follows is true,
except for the plot

CHAPTER 1

Serge Willoughby just wanted to make money and have fun. He didn't mean to start World War III.

It began, as many calamities do, at a Washington party, in this case a gathering of the national security community—a deceptively collegial term for the flock of officers, spies, and corporate mavens that formed what was known in less euphemistic times as the military-industrial complex.

Willoughby came to these parties because he had to. For he was a consultant, someone who made considerable sums of money by solving problems that his clients—mainly the military services and the weapons manufacturers—couldn't solve by themselves, or, rather, couldn't solve in a way that convinced the budget-masters in the Pentagon or Congress to buy their wares. In short, a good consultant—and Willoughby was one of the best—supplied the veneer of intellectual heft and mathematical precision that clients needed in order to boost their fortunes or, in some cases, stay alive. And these parties were where the gossip first circulated on which big weapons programs were in the lineup, who would be the sources of resistance, and what sorts of arguments might alter their views.

So, Willoughby walked into this particular party, on a warm, early autumn Sunday evening, in a characteristically blasé disposition, as if nothing was out of the ordinary and the world wasn't about to take a cataclysmic turn. He looked around the expansive living room and saw that the guests had coalesced into the usual tribal pattern. Huddled in one corner were the intelligence analysts: expressionless, bedecked in suits that were perpetually out of fashion (which, in this season, meant wide lapels and diagonally striped ties), whispering to one another through the corners of their mouths in codewords and acronyms that no one else in the room knew existed. Nearby were the foreign diplomats, more colorful in couture and demeanor, chuckling about some breach of esoteric protocol, one of them sauntering over to the spooks' corner for a brief exchange, a clear sign that he was the undercover spy at his embassy. Spanning the middle of the room, with nothing to hide, were the lobbyists and the defense contractors, exchanging phone numbers, setting lunch dates, grabbing the shoulder of a congressman or midlevel Pentagon official, crisscrossing the room from the wine-and-booze bar to the fruit-and-nuts bowls to the cracker-and-cheese board and back again, pitching, pleading, and kowtowing to would-be customers.

Willoughby, who routinely flitted among all these clans with equal parts familiarity and disaffection, was mulling which way to turn when a Navy vice admiral approached him.

"Serge!" he called out in high spirits. "You'll be getting the contract for that analysis tomorrow. And listen, the chief wants no surprises."

"Only two things would surprise me," Willoughby coolly replied. "First, if any of you guys in the Pentagon *wanted* surprises. Second, if you ever paid my bills on time."

Willoughby moved toward the wine table but was intercepted by an aerospace executive. "Hey, Serge," he said with brow-furrowed seriousness, "are you going to bid for that study on the cost-effectiveness of a shoulder-fired hypersonic glide vehicle?"

Willoughby grunted. "I do stupid, and I do science fiction," he said, "but I don't do stupid science fiction."

He resumed his course toward the booze, but was blocked again, this time by a young man who introduced himself as the newly appointed deputy to the assistant to the deputy assistant secretary of defense. "Dr. Willoughby," the young man said with a slight stutter, averting his gaze, as if nervous to be addressing a great sage directly, "what do you think of the new report concluding that North Korea will acquire a nuclear first-strike capability within three years?"

"It's preposterous," Willoughby replied.

"But it's a *classified* report," the deputy to the assistant to the deputy assistant insisted.

"Here's something to keep in mind," Willoughby lectured in a tone of timeworn wisdom. "Just because something is classified doesn't mean it's true."

It was a line that Willoughby had recited many times to eager initiates in the field. He was slightly annoyed that it always prompted a laugh, as if he were joking.

A few years ago, Willoughby would have enjoyed all this banter and attention. But he was growing weary of these soirées. The guests were so boringly self-regarding, so narrow yet so convinced that their stamps of exclusivity—the high-level security clearances that most of them held—instilled them with special knowledge of how the world worked. And the repetition was getting brain-numbing: they were, more and more, the same people he'd seen at these parties for years now, or, if not the same individuals, then the same types, as if churned through some DNA-sequencing machine from generation to generation. In the old days, some of the men would bring their wives, and, when Willoughby had a chance, he would talk with them, which, it seemed, was more than their husbands ever did. But the wives had long ago stopped coming to these outings, no doubt having better things to do. In recent years, a fair number of women had joined the defense community and become think-tank analysts, senior officials, even consultants, but they seemed to avoid parties like these. Willoughby wondered: did they throw their own parties, and, if so, were they more interesting than those of the boys' club? Was there any way he could get invited, even on a onetime guest pass?

Willoughby was particularly annoyed about this party—his mood was more dour than usual, his replies to fellow guests more abrupt—because it was taking place in the Georgetown townhouse of Wolf Mandelbaum, an older consultant, lionized as a giant in the field, a living legend: a myth played up, most of all, by Mandelbaum himself. By now, everyone in the business had heard of the epic study that Mandelbaum wrote and then briefed *ninety-three times*, to allegedly spellbound audiences, including, on one occasion, a sitting vice president of the United States. Willoughby was stunned that this tale still impressed so many of his colleagues. The study was a 186-page opus with sixty-seven color-coded charts (his followers would rattle off these figures with the same breathlessness as their ooh-ing and ah-ing over the ninety-three briefings), which concluded that the Russians were well on their way to launching anti-missile laser weapons into outer space—an assessment that, no one seemed to recall, turned out to be utterly false. This wasn't such a sin by itself;

everybody gets things wrong sometimes. What made the study—and its author—irredeemable to Willoughby was that the *math* was bad: equations were improperly applied, basic arithmetic incorrectly calculated, data simply invented. It was one thing to twist a problem in a way to get the answer that your client wanted; all consultants did that to some degree. But to get the right answer by *concocting* the numbers—that was beyond the pale.

Mandelbaum did exude a charisma, a patina of cosmopolitanism, rare and thus greatly admired or envied in his circle: the Italian suits, the fine wines, the gourmet food prepared and fastidiously presented by his charming but shy Korean wife, Chae-won, who spent most of her time at his parties cooking in the kitchen, replenishing the food-and-drink tables, greeting guests with a warm smile, and, on her way back to the oven, whispering something to Wolf, who would solemnly nod.

It was comical, in Mandelbaum's heyday, back in the 1990s, to watch his pack of acolytes at the think tank he briefly ran—the Harbinger Corporation—frittering away their slender salaries on tailored duds and vintage reserves, urging their wives to become gourmet cooks, just like Chae-won, thinking that if they mastered these arts of fine living, they might become the Wolf Mandelbaums of their generation.

Everyone also seemed to have forgotten that Mandelbaum's enterprise went up in smoke nearly a decade ago, after he took his principal donor out for breakfast at a fashionable, perpetually crowded diner that took no reservations—the line was long, it would take an hour to get in, the donor, starving, suggested they go elsewhere, but Wolf told him, in his continental cadence and condescending tone, "It is my goal in life not to consume a single inferior calorie." And that was it: the donor didn't renew his contract (which is what the two had set out that morning to sign and celebrate), and no one knew quite where Mandelbaum was getting his money these days.

Willoughby glanced over at his host, who was surrounded by a gaggle of young congressional staffers—a handful were always invited to these parties, so they could make contacts and absorb how a defense-policy intellectual should behave—all huddled over a fondue pot, riveted as he instructed them in the art of optimizing the amount of melted cheese to ladle over the bread crusts. Willoughby, who'd seen this routine before, rolled his eyes. The man's arrogance and mendacity corroded everything around him. Then he heard Mandelbaum say, "When I briefed the vice president on the laser-weapons study…"—as if the study had been some succès d'éstime, the briefing his entrée to the corridors of power—and, suddenly, a synapse snapped in Willoughby's brain, the mad tang of venom dripped down his throat.

Willoughby had had enough.

He slipped out of the living room, down the hallway, up the stairs, and into his host's office ("the Wolf den," Mandelbaum liked to call it, in a lame bit of wordplay). It was a designer's overreach that Willoughby had surveyed once before, back when the two were friendly: the antique French desk with the Eames chair and the Tiffany lamp, the black silk wallpaper, the row of tall mahogany bookcases jammed with law volumes (though Mandelbaum had never studied law) and leather-bound classics (a few expensive collectibles, but mostly mail-order knockoffs, their pages— Willoughby had once inspected them—unthumbed). He sat at the desk (it *was* a comfortable chair), picked up the phone, and did something unspeakably nasty.

A few nights earlier, Willoughby had gone out for dinner with Chas Greenway, a friend and classmate from long-ago graduate-school days who now worked at Tailored Access Operations, the elite hacker unit of the National Security Agency. As the dinner spilled over into drinks, Greenway, deeply wasted, started bragging about his latest project. Barely able to contain his triumph, he confided that he'd been working with a covert counterintelligence unit of the FBI, which was tracking a crew of Chinese sleeper agents in the Washington area, and that, after months of diligent digging, he had retrieved the phone number that many of these agents were periodically calling. It was the number of a hardware store in suburban Maryland. Judging by the messages they left, the spies seemed to be ordering various tools, but in fact they were reciting codes, which were passed on to a handler in Berlin, who then transmitted them to Beijing. More recently still, Greenway and his fellow hackers at NSA headquarters in Fort Meade, only a few miles from the hardware store, had traced these calls to their sources— some of the sleepers were phoning the store on open lines, so certain were they of eluding detection, perhaps figuring that the NSA had ceased the old-school business of tapping phones in the age of cyber espionage—and now, the bureau was starting to round them up. A couple of them had been flipped to our side (they enjoyed their American lifestyles and had no desire to get shipped back to China, where their carelessness would get them demoted or locked up), and the agency was using them to send disinformation to their unsuspecting masters.

Then Greenway, chortling with increasingly drunken glee as his story progressed, did something that shocked even Willoughby: he rattled off the hardware store's phone number.

Willoughby's first reaction was to wonder when his friend had last passed a security exam. Could the NSA really be so negligent as to expose its latest set of crown jewels to a blatant alcoholic? His second reaction was to repeat the phone number in his head over and over until he memorized it. When he got home that night, he jotted it down on a scrap of paper, which he then folded and tucked into the middle of a dense tome on guerrilla warfare in ancient Rome, which no visitor, invited or otherwise, would think to flip through. Days later, the number still flashed in his brain like a neon sign.

So now, Willoughby picked up the phone—Mandelbaum's phone—and dialed that number. When the answering machine beeped, he loosened his vocal cords, managed a decent impersonation of his host's supercilious baritone, and improvised a request for some antique tools: a John Deere wrench, a Leonard Bailey bronze scraper, and an Ohio No. 1C smoothing plane. He knew such esoterica from a summer job in his youth, decades ago, as an apprentice to a carpenter who was obsessed with high-end gadgetry. But those listening in on the call would likely assume that he was speaking in code. And maybe, a day or two hence, some federal agents would pay Mandelbaum a visit, flash their badges, and ask some rude questions about where his loyalties lay—make him nervous, shake the stuffing out of his vaunted self-confidence.

Mandelbaum would deserve it. He was such an asshole.

Willoughby came by his cynicism honestly.

His parents, nice kids who'd grown up in a small Midwestern town, went off to the University of Wisconsin, studied American history, and took their readings on US imperialism as a traumatic rebuke to everything about their lives up till then. In response, they joined an anarcho-syndicalist collective, which is where Serge—named after Victor Serge, the Russian Trotskyist and author of *Memoirs of a Revolutionary*—spent much of his childhood. It was his own form of adolescent rebellion to immerse himself in mathematics and win a scholarship to M.I.T. at age 15. He graduated in short order, then earned a Ph.D. from its political science department, specializing in defense and arms-control studies, and after that, owing to a stellar recommendation from a highly respected professor, nabbed a job as a junior staff member on the House Armed Services Committee in Washington.

It was a heady experience for the precocious Willoughby: poring over military budgets, scrutinizing hundreds of line items for their cost-effectiveness and consistency with national strategy, slashing or seeking alternatives to the programs that didn't make the grade. He viewed the job as an affirmation of his academic work—of the bedrock premise that quantitative analysis could play a serious, even foundational role in national security policymaking. And Willoughby proved to be brilliantly cut out for his new career, parsing the essentials from impenetrable documents in record time and drafting summaries—talking point memos for his bosses, the lawmakers—of impressive comprehensiveness and clarity.

Then came his existential unraveling. The MX missile was the big item in the Defense Department's annual budget back then, the topic of marathon debates in both houses of Congress. It was an enormous missile, the largest, most powerful, and most accurate nuclear-tipped missile that the American military had ever developed.

But the main thing about the MX—which, around this time, was renamed the Peacekeeper (such a clueless irony that even the somber young Willoughby found it hilarious)—was that it would be a *mobile* missile. The Soviets were building their own giant missiles, which could theoretically destroy America's current land-based missiles, known as the Minutemen, as they stood on spring-loaded platforms in their underground silos. The US Air Force, the Peacekeeper's funder, hadn't yet decided *how* to move the MX around. Consultants of the day had drawn up several blueprints—for moving them by road, by rail, by airplane, by tunnels—each more gargantuan and impractical than the one before. Still, the debate raged on, the hawks arguing. that the Minutemen faced a "window of vulnerability" in the next five years, so the Peacekeepers had to be built right away. The doves countered that the Minutemen weren't so vulnerable (some calculations suggested that Soviet missiles weren't as accurate as the hawks claimed), and, even if they were, it didn't matter because most of America's nuclear weapons were loaded onto submarines, which quietly roamed beneath the ocean's surface, undetectable and thus invulnerable, meaning that, in the event of a Soviet first strike on the Minuteman silos, the US could retaliate with the submarine-launched missiles—and since the Soviets knew this, they wouldn't launch a first strike to begin with.

Willoughby took no side in this argument. The cases on both sides—the hawks and the doves—struck him as logical, backed up by intelligence data. He assumed that everyone involved was debating in good faith. He found the whole business stimulating.

Then, in his first term, President Ronald Reagan concluded that all of the mobile schemes were crazy and decided simply to stuff the Peacekeepers into existing Minuteman silos. And then something weird happened. The doves started arguing that Reagan's plan was a terrible idea because those silos were vulnerable to a Soviet first strike. And the hawks started arguing that, actually, the silos weren't so vulnerable, and, even if they were, it didn't matter because the US could retaliate with missiles launched from submarines.

In other words, the legislators on each side pulled a complete 180, adopting the arguments that the other side had been making in order to retain their original position on whether or not to build the new missile. The shallowness and hypocrisy were blatant, all the more so as everyone pretended not to notice. Both sides kept debating, with no less passion or conviction than before, as if their rationales hadn't changed at all, much less flipped diametrically. The crude, simple truth was this: the hawks wanted an expensive, big, new missile— the doves didn't. Logic, math, and strategy had nothing to do with any of it. The appearance that they did was a pretense.

Willoughby walked out of the House chamber that day desolate. The session he'd just witnessed was traumatic, his first close-up experience with intellectual dishonesty. Then he heard someone yell out, "Hey, young Willoughby!"

He looked up.

The shout came from Giles Molloy, who was ambling down the steps from the spectators' gallery and headed Willoughby's way. Molloy was the first professional defense consultant Willoughby had ever met. He was in his mid-30s, a dozen or so years older than Willoughby, short, lean, fast-walking, fast-talking, dressed in a seersucker sport jacket and khaki trousers regardless of the weather, approaching every spectacle in life with a sly grin and a cocked eyebrow.

"*That* was fun." Molloy chuckled.

"It was *disgusting!*" Willoughby replied. He was so disgusted, he might have to quit his job, go into another profession, maybe admit that his hippie-anarchist parents were right.

Molloy howled with laughter. "What do you think, these guys base their votes on rational analysis?" he crowed. His face turned serious. "You're a smart kid. You need to get out of this *place*, but don't get out of the *game*." He paused. "You know what you should do?"

Willoughby shook his head, still downtrodden, though raising his eyebrows in a sign of tentative curiosity.

"You should become a consultant," Molloy said. "You should be like me."

Molloy was one of the few consultants in town who had a sense of humor about himself or his trade. He called his company Plan B

Enterprises ("because," as he once told Willoughby, "there *is* no Plan A"), and joked, though never within a client's earshot, that his firm's motto should be "We're not happy until you're not happy."

The two walked to the Tune Inn, Molloy's favorite dive bar. It was located a few blocks off most congressional staffers' beaten path of watering holes and, as an added bonus, served up juicier burgers and stronger drinks.

"So," Molloy began his pep talk soon after they sat down and ordered, "you learned today that nobody gives a shit about your fine-tuned analyses. They like what they like and don't like what they don't like for their own reasons. Maybe it's their guts or their campaign donations or jobs back home, what gets them reelected, what gets them laid, who knows what reasons. So why do they need guys like you and me to churn out our detailed studies? Because they don't want to seem like greedy cavemen. They want to *look* as though they've reached their conclusions after deep research and rigorous reflection. They need guys like us, so the *citizenry* will think that they're not just making this shit up as they go—that they've got a grip on the ins and outs of war and peace, and we're not all going to wake up some morning, look out the window, and see a mushroom cloud billowing up through the sky.

"And by the way," Molloy went on, taking another gulp from his beer, then a chaser of scotch, "I'm not talking just about your bosses on the Hill. This goes for highflyers in the executive branch, too. In fact, *that's* how my profession got started."

He launched into a history lecture, which he'd recited to a few other youngsters shimmying up the ropes.

"It was all McNamara's doing," he began. "Robert Strange McNamara, John Kennedy's secretary of defense. Brilliant guy, in his early forties, youngest president of Ford Motors, he brought in a team of old classmates from the Harvard Business School—'whiz kids,' they called themselves—who went over the books with 'systems analysis,' their phrase for high-level statistics, and overhauled the whole company. Kennedy hired him to do the same at the Pentagon. The brass had pissed away money on all kinds of junk, multiple redundancies, tons of waste. They'd told presidents and congressmen that it was all *required for national security*, and who were these *civilians* to challenge this row of decorated generals and admirals? McNamara came in, looked at the test records, saw what worked, what didn't, calculated which of the redundant weapons killed the highest number of bad guys for the same amount of money, or killed the same number of bad guys for the least amount of money, and he slashed the losers—he *eliminated* major weapons systems!

Willoughby sat riveted. He'd vaguely heard about McNamara and the whiz kids, but hadn't known the backdrop, the political origins tale of his own brand of defense analysis, which had seemed so pristine back in grad school.

"Well," Molloy went on, picking up steam and munching on an onion ring, "the brass were *shocked*. They'd never seen anything like this. They didn't know how to handle this guy, they didn't know what 'systems analysis' *was*."

Molloy downed another chaser. "So," he wrapped up his seminar, "the generals and the admirals hired *consultants*, guys with advanced degrees in math who could help them fight back with their *own* systems analysis, coming up with equations and charts and all the rest, showing that the officers' favorite weapons were the *optimal* systems, *cost-effective*, the proverbial cat's pajamas. And it's been like that ever since: the Joint Chiefs fighting the Pentagon civilians, the Air Force fighting the Navy, the Navy fighting the Army—back and forth, back and forth, and the consultants swelling in number, swelling in stature, swelling with *money*."

At that last word, Molloy cupped his hand and rubbed his thumb against his index finger. Then he paused and opened his eyes wide. "I've got an idea on how you could make your mark in the business," he exclaimed, slapping his young friend on the shoulder. "You know all the arguments on both sides of every issue in the defense world, and you know them as well as anybody. Take this ridiculous MX debate. You could have written the study that says the Minuteman is vulnerable, we need a new mobile missile—*and* you could have written the study that says the Minuteman is just fine and all the mobile schemes are nuts. You could have written the first study for the Air Force, which wants as many MX missiles as the factories can churn out. You could have written the second study for the Navy, which wants Congress and the president to believe that all we need are submarines and we can get rid of Air Force missiles altogether. On every budget fight going on," Molloy concluded with a note of triumph, "you could work both sides of the street and make double the money."

Willoughby sat up. "Janus," he muttered.

"What?"

"Janus," he repeated, "the Roman god with two faces. That's what I'll call my consulting firm—the Janus Corporation."

Molloy thought a few seconds. "Nice, very clever," he said. "And don't worry, none of your clients will get the literary reference. Even if they did, they wouldn't care about your two faces, as long as you at least pretend to be *personally* neutral."

"That won't be a problem," Willoughby replied coldly. After that afternoon's debate in the House, he didn't believe in anything.

Forty years had passed since that life-changing twilight at the Tune Inn. Willoughby was barely 21 back then—his fellow staff members called him "Wunderkind," a few of them affectionately—and now he was a shade past 60. The Janus Corporation was still a thriving business.

His reputation had soared with his first contract, which acquired legendary status as "the bomber caper." There was, when he started out, a faction of the Air Force still enchanted with bombers and the derring-do of pilots in scarves steering big airplanes under the enemy's radar, practically hugging the ground, dropping their nuclear payload on a target, then whooshing up and away to dodge the blast wave. The denizens of this faction—the Fly Boys, some called them—had never taken to intercontinental ballistic missiles; they couldn't conceive the tedium of sitting inside a concrete hole in the ground, waiting for an order to launch, pushing a button, then probably getting incinerated themselves a half-hour later when the Soviets retaliated. What kind of job was that for an *Air Force* officer? They'd heard about Willoughby's disenchantment with the MX debate (he always suspected Molloy had passed along his name with an enthusiastic recommendation), so they offered him a contract.

They wanted their Pentagon overlords to fund a new bomber, but couldn't contrive a good sales pitch. Bombers were seen as old hat, and *penetrating* bombers—planes that flew across enemy lines, evaded antiaircraft batteries, and dropped the Big One right on the target—were considered obsolete. The current fleet of B–52 bombers had been built all too ruggedly: they'd been around for decades, would likely last for decades longer, and some of them were now armed with small, accurate *cruise* missiles, which could be fired as far as fifteen-hundred miles away from the target—well outside Soviet territory, so there was no need for the plane to maneuver around or under air defenses. The other services, and even some of the younger Air Force officers, were telling the Fly Boys to join the late twentieth century. It was crazy, they said, to fuel an arms race with a new weapon that had no real rationale.

When Willoughby heard the pitch, only a couple weeks after his great disillusion, he shrugged and replied, "*No* new weapon has a real rationale. What's wrong with that?"

The colonel who brought him the proposal laughed, but Willoughby was morosely serious.

It took Willoughby only a few days to write a report that solved the Fly Boys' problem. He briefed it to their "strategy group"—a one-star general, two colonels, and four majors—crammed in a small windowless conference room in a remote corridor of the Pentagon basement.

"The mission of this new bomber," Willoughby began in a clipped tone that lent him gravitas beyond his years, "is not to win a nuclear war, which, let's face it, isn't likely to happen anyway. The mission is to win the *arms race*. Yes, a new bomber will cost us a lot of money, but to shoot it down, the Soviets will have to spend a lot *more* money on air-defense weapons. The Soviets are strapped. Their budget is as tight as a clam. Every ruble they spend on *defense* is a ruble they can't spend on *offense*. The new bomber will *leverage* us into a *strategic* advantage. It will force the enemy into bankruptcy."

He walked over to the blackboard and scribbled a slew of equations with blazing speed and bold clarity (this was before the days of PowerPoint), showing precisely how much money the Soviets would need to spend and by what year they'd go bust.

When he finished, the Fly Boys gave him a standing ovation.

After returning to his office, Willoughby phoned a Navy officer he'd met during the MX debate on the Hill—he knew the Navy was in a fierce budget battle with the Air Force—and told him what the Fly Boys were cooking up. A few days later, he won a contract to write a report showing why a new bomber would be a bad idea. He argued that cruise missiles made a penetrating bomber unnecessary. He also altered a few of the assumptions in his Air Force study to show that the Soviets could improve their air defenses without going bankrupt. (Willoughby wasn't *making up* numbers. The intelligence agencies had published a *range* of estimates on the health of the Soviet economy. He used the gloomiest estimate for the Air Force study and the brightest estimate for the Navy study.) Finally, as a bonus and almost as a prank, more to see if he could get away with it than out of any conviction, he scribbled some equations showing that cruise missiles launched from Navy ships or submarines would be more cost-effective than cruise missiles launched from Air Force B-52s.

Both sets of clients were pleased. The Pentagon higher-ups loved the idea of "leveraging" the Kremlin in an offense-defense arms race, so the Air Force got its new bomber. And the Navy officers got money to develop a new sea-launched cruise missile, even though they'd never even thought to ask for one.

These were the lessons Willoughby absorbed for the months and years to come: first, nobody in Washington really believed anything—rather, they contrived their beliefs to fit their vested interests. Second, a skillfully presented, mathematically grounded argument for a new weapon, almost *any* new weapon, was likely to convince the higher-ups—and to generate more business for the Janus Corporation.

Halcyon days! Long ago, only a few years after setting up shop, Willoughby had earned enough money to ditch his cubbyhole of an office just off an exit from the Capital Beltway, the interstate ringing the outskirts of D.C., where most consultants hung their shingle (hence the term ascribed to many of them: "Beltway Bandits"), and to rent a cozy but high-ceilinged space in the city, just off DuPont Circle, so that he could take strolls, sit in the park, visit an art gallery, or browse through a bookstore on his lunch breaks. Not long after that move, he bought a penthouse condo in The Wyoming, a much-desired Beaux Arts apartment building a few blocks north of his new office, so that he could walk to work.

Willoughby still enjoyed the *process* of his enterprise—pitching an idea, conjuring its opposite and pitching it as well, chasing the contracts for both, devising an elegant mathematical framework for the broader problem, crunching the numbers to fit the pre-cooked answers, drafting the voluminous reports, and finally presenting the summaries in a theatrical lecture to the clients. But he long ago lost what interest he'd ever had in the *substance* of the job. Though he gave his analytic all to whatever position his clients paid him to take, he was genuinely indifferent to the outcome—which clients won a Pentagon contract or which side of an argument was true, if there was such a thing as truth.

He kept his consulting firm deliberately small, avoiding the rat race of hiring more staff in order to chase more work, then having to chase more work in order to pay the staff. He did most of the analysis and writing by himself. He employed only a business manager, who doubled as a receptionist, and two research assistants, who perused the trade journals, congressional hearings, and other sources of gossip and news to inspire ideas for more studies and contracts. He treated his staff well, even jovially when appropriate, paid them a bit more than the industry standard, and let the especially talented assistants help out on a study, giving them some seasoning, a credit, and the foundations for a lavish letter of recommendation when they departed for a more creative or lucrative job.

His aversion to commitment permeated his personal life as well. He dallied in romantic affairs: several lasted for months; a few stretched into a year or longer. But he never married. Washington was a great city for finding attractive, intelligent women whose careers encouraged a similar disinclination to settling down.

And so, he set out simply to enjoy his life as much as he could. He valued his leisure time. Each year, he bought season tickets to the Wizards basketball games (usually taking a client) and to Jason Moran's jazz series at the Kennedy Center (usually going alone). He often dined out with friends, male and female. He traveled when he could, in the spring or the fall, to one of his favorite cities in Europe (London, Paris, Rome, Berlin), and, every few months, to New York, where he savored the museums and galleries, saw a play, took in a set at the Village Vanguard or the Comedy Cellar, bringing along the woman he was seeing, if he was seeing one, or, if he wasn't, traveling solo, as a flañeur, a walker in the city, either way escaping the Washington drear of policy, power, and politics.

Not that life at home was so bad. He still had his hair, speckled a salt-and-pepper gray, which lent a debonair sheen to his otherwise ordinary looks—so ordinary that, several years ago, before the distinguishing gray streaks set in, Chas Greenway advised him to take up robbing banks, as no witness to his crimes could supply police department sketch-artists with an even slightly useful description ("medium height, medium build, no limps or remarkable facial features…"). Even now, he was still in decent shape, though his daily workout regimen had slackened to three times a week, or sometimes, these days, just two. He'd fashioned his apartment into a cozy retreat, flush with books, records, art, antique rugs, and fine furniture—the material expression of aesthetically driven shopping expeditions spanning decades. Each morning, he rose from a restful sleep (he'd never had trouble sleeping), stretched his arms while roaring a yawn, gazed out his bedroom window across a panoramic view of the nation's capital, and recited only half-sarcastically the epithet that he wanted inscribed on his tombstone: "Another day in fucking paradise."

The morning after the party at Wolf Mandelbaum's house, he woke up feeling a bit unsettled. He hadn't drunk much or eaten anything awful (say what you will about Wolf, the food at his parties was excellent), but he'd probably gone too far with the prank on the telephone, calling the number of the Chinese spy line that the NSA was monitoring not just despite the fact, but in the hope, that his host would wind up in trouble with the feds. Willoughby shook off the dread, assuring himself that the spoof wasn't likely to provoke an incident; he knew of some wiretap cases where the taps were never monitored. Besides, *some* of the phone calls to this hardware store must come from real customers; the call that he made from Wolf's den might be interpreted as one of those. There was no reason why some FBI agents, if they were listening in, would assume that the caller *had* to be a Chinese spy.

Anyway, Willoughby decided to take it easy that morning. Giles Molloy, his old mentor, had recently announced his retirement—he'd turned 75 and decided enough was enough—and he was circulating the most promising job applications from his files. One of Willoughby's assistants had quit a few weeks earlier, so Molloy sent him one of the résumés, attaching a note: "This guy reminds me of you at his age." So, Willoughby had arranged an interview in his office for that day at noon.

He phoned his secretary, Donna Cappella. He'd hired her a few years earlier, for oddly capricious reasons. At first sight, she seemed all wrong for the job: bouffant hairdo, cat eyes glasses, tattoos swirling up both arms, perpetually disinterested expression. But he liked her name—it sang to him, both in print and spoken out loud—so he gave her a chance (something that, he found out later, no one else in this staid town had done), and she turned out to be a jewel: very smart, competent, resourceful, industrious. It was a typical sight, whenever he stepped out of his office into the reception area, to see her working on all three of her computer screens, her eyes flitting back and forth from one to the others, while simultaneously carrying on a detailed, sometimes technical conversation on the telephone.

One of Willoughby's two assistant jobs came open soon after Donna Cappella came onboard, and he decided to make his choice on the same criteria, which led him to hire a pudgy slob named Manny Slaughter—a great name, he thought, for someone in the war business—who also turned out to be a major find, a search-engine genius.

"Good morning, Donna Cappella," Willoughby said when she picked up the phone. "I'm expecting a job applicant to come by for an interview, a young man named"—he paused to look again at the resume—"Vijay Gupta."

"He's already here," she said. It was a half hour before the designated time.

"He's one of Molloy's picks. What's he like?"

"He seems very earnest."

"Hmmm. Maybe we'll wring that out of him. I'll be there soon."

Willoughby hung up and looked again at Gupta's CV. Good credentials: born and raised in Washington DC to a family of immigrant physicians from New Delhi; degrees from Stanford; a year at the RAND Corporation, where he wrote two monographs, *A Data Compendium on Worldwide Air and Maritime Forces* and *The Influence of Cyber Technologies on the Strategic Nuclear Balance*—not exactly page-turners, but just the sorts of green-eyeshade works that an aspiring research assistant at the Janus Corporation would plausibly churn out.

He stumbled out of his apartment and took the half-mile downhill stroll to his office, arriving just before noon. Gupta was in the waiting room, thumbs wailing away on his iPhone. He was tall and scrawny, dressed in grey with wire-rimmed glasses, also grey—the sort of young man who, in an earlier era, would have worn a pen protector in his shirt pocket and a slide rule on his belt. Willoughby introduced himself. They shook hands, then walked into the conference room, a rectangle with the window shades pulled down, a six-foot-long table in the middle flanked by a half-dozen oak library chairs, one wall lined with file cabinets, the others with overstuffed bookcases.

"Mr. Gupta," Willoughby began. "I've heard impressive things about you. Who's your favorite poet?"

Molloy had long ago taught Willoughby to ask this question of all job seekers, first to rattle them a bit, but more to see if they had any outside interests, on the assumption that, if they didn't, the job was likely to drive them nuts.

"Umm, Auden?" Gupta replied, in a soft, rising inflection, a bit too waveringly, but it was a good choice.

"Let me present you with a problem," Willoughby went on. "I received a letter the other day from our military's top admiral, the chief of naval operations. As you know, this administration wants to get out of the Middle East and cut the defense budget. So, according to the letter, the secretary of defense has asked the chief how many aircraft carriers the Navy would need if the United States decided to remove all of its military forces from the Persian Gulf. As you no doubt know, the Navy now has ten aircraft carriers, two of which are committed to the Persian Gulf. The chief wants *me* to answer the secretary's question. How would *you* answer it?"

"Well," Gupta replied, "first I'd say this is a *terrible* idea…"

"No," Willoughby interrupted. "That's not the assignment. The top civilian in the Department of Defense doesn't care what the Navy's top admiral thinks of the *idea*, which probably came directly from the president of the United States. He wants to know how many carriers the country would need *if* we abandoned the Persian Gulf. What's your answer *to that?*"

"I guess the answer is eight," Gupta said. "Ten carriers, take away two, that equals eight."

"No," Willoughby said. "The correct answer is ten."

"But the math…"

"The correct answer is *always* ten," Willoughby said, calm but firm. "Aircraft carriers are the centerpiece of the Navy. The number of carriers drives the number of all other ships."

"Yes, I know," Gupta said. "Each carrier strike group has an aircraft carrier, two guided missile cruisers, two destroyers, a frigate, usually two submarines, and a supply ship. The loss of two carriers would mean the loss of"—he took less than a second to add up the numbers, clearly eager to show off a few of the facts at his nimble fingertips—"sixteen additional boats."

"Ah, you get it," Willoughby responded. "So, if the secretary of defense wants to know how many aircraft carriers we'd need if he scrapped the rest of our arsenal and chopped all the tanks and missiles into tiny bits of scrap metal, the right answer is *still* ten. If the messiah came back, lions lay down with lambs, and the world's leaders banged their swords into plowshares, the right answer is still...?" Willoughby let Gupta fill in the blank.

"Ten?" he said, hesitantly.

"Exactly," Willoughby said.

Gupta still seemed puzzled.

"Look," Willoughby explained. "I *know* the secretary of defense and the chief of naval operations. They're not idiots. They know that ten minus two equals eight. The chief wants a study—a big ream of paper—that proves he needs ten aircraft carriers, no matter what the secretary throws at him. And the secretary—who's not exactly keen on unilateral disarmament, either—wants the same big ream of paper to prove the same point to the clever boys and girls on the White House staff who probably put him up to this."

"But how would you *go about* making that point?" Gupta asked, with seemingly genuine curiosity.

"*Now* you're getting the idea," Willoughby replied. "Well, I don't know. I just got this letter. But it's not exactly rocket science. We could put together a study that concludes something like, 'Removing the Persian Gulf as an area of operation allows the transfer of naval assets to the Indo-Pacific region, where current deployments are inadequate to fulfill mission requirements.' That gives one of the exiled carriers something to do. As for the other, we could say, 'Due to the advanced age of the current fleet and shortages in personnel, all carriers must spend longer times in port for repairs and maintenance, thus requiring one additional carrier to be at sea at all times.' Get it?" Willoughby summed up. "Ten minus two, plus two, equals ten."

"Interesting," Gupta observed, nodding his head slowly.

It seemed to Willoughby that the young applicant didn't quite know whether this was the path he wanted to carve in life. It might take him a few more years and a few hard hits to reach that moment of epiphany, or maybe he'd opt for the intellectual purity of think tanks and academia.

After Gupta left, Willoughby phoned his old mentor. "So, how'd my guy do?" Molloy asked.

"His favorite poet is Auden," Willoughby said.

"I might have given him a heads up on that," Molloy admitted sheepishly.

"I thought you might have."

"Did he remind you a bit of yourself?"

"Maybe a bit of me *before* the Tune Inn conversion. I don't know, I'll consider him. Thanks for the tip."

"Hey, before you go," Molloy said. "You were at Wolf Mandelbaum's party last night, right?"

"Yeah."

"Did anything strange go on?"

Willoughby hesitated. "I don't think so. What do you have in mind?"

"Wolf has been arrested," Molloy said.

"What?"

"Yeah, I'm told a caravan of black sedans screeched up to his house early this morning, sirens blazing. Feds jump out, pistols drawn, they knock on the door, Wolf opens it, they surround him, cuff him, take him downtown, the whole bit."

"How's Chae-won taking this?" Willoughby asked.

"They arrested her too. As an accomplice."

"An accomplice to what?"

"Word on the street," Molloy replied, "is they're detained on charges of *espionage*."

Willoughby audibly gulped. "Listen, Giles, I've got to go, I'll call you later."

He slumped into his chair. "Holy shit," he muttered. For maybe the first time in a long life of mischief and merriment, Willoughby knew that he'd plunged himself into serious trouble.

CHAPTER 2

Five minutes later, Willoughby was still slumped, frozen in a catatonic state, the likes of which he had never before experienced, his eyes locked to a distant blur, his mind emptied of sensible content.

The yelp of a police siren down on the street, five stories below, snapped him out of his stupor. He leapt out of his chair and rubbed his skull, as if to prod the synapses back into functioning. Once fully revived, he pulled the cell phone out of his pocket and sent a text to his loose-lipped pal, Chas Greenway, arranging a rendezvous for that evening. He had to learn more about the wiretap on the Maryland hardware store. What were the Chinese spies up to? How incriminating was the mere fact of a phone call to the store? How much trouble was Mandelbaum facing? And if the FBI or NSA analyzed the voice on the call from Mandelbaum's phone, how much trouble might *Willoughby* soon face?

They met at a rooftop restaurant in Adams Morgan, near Willoughby's apartment: too urban to attract any of Greenway's Fort Meade colleagues, too posh for any of the neighborhood's left-wing activists, who might take notes upon overhearing stray bits of what would seem to be a classified conversation.

Greenway arrived only a few minutes later than scheduled, his tie loose, hair unkempt, belly in need of a size larger suit jacket. Willoughby was already waiting at a table as far away from the other diners as the maître d' could manage. After they ordered drinks, he got straight to the point. "Listen, Chas, the phone number of this hardware store in Maryland…"

"*What* hardware store?" Greenway interrupted.

"You know," Willoughby replied, lowering his voice to nearly a whisper, "the hardware store that the Chinese spies are phoning."

"Who told you about that?" Greenway yelled, his eyes widening.

"What do you mean?" Willoughby said. "*You* told me about that."

"I did no such fucking thing!" Greenway shot back, shaking. He looked all around—behind him, off to the side, under the table, out the rooftop balcony to the windows of the buildings across the street. "Did security put you up to this? Is this a test? Are you wired?"

Willoughby sat, numbed. Greenway wasn't pretending; the fear and trembling were clearly real. Had he drunk so much at their dinner a mere week ago that he *blacked out*, erasing all memory of the conversation, if he'd formed a memory of it to begin with?

"I can't stay here, I can't talk about this," Greenway mumbled. He got up and dashed out, not even waiting for his drink, a capper to this startling turn of events, as Greenway was known to wait out all manner of awkward moments in order to down an alcoholic beverage.

Now Willoughby didn't know where to turn. Very few people in his circle would know about an ongoing intelligence operation, and if he brought it up with any of them, they would wonder how *he* knew about it. (Willoughby had a Top Secret security clearance, but this sort of thing was classified way beyond Top Secret.) Even if they didn't report him to the feds (a distinct possibility), they would refuse to answer his questions and, as Greenway had done, walk away.

Willoughby considered, very reluctantly, calling a journalist. He didn't like dealing with reporters, didn't trust them. The few times he'd helped them out, early in his career, when they called him with questions, usually about technical issues regarding a high-profile weapon system, he ended up regretting it. The articles they published weren't quite *wrong*, but they missed or misstated important details, or they twisted the information he'd given them into a different story from the one he was trying to pitch. The articles didn't damage him personally; he always spoke on background, so he was never identified by name. Still, why help someone with an agenda that wasn't his own? What a waste of time. Also, Willoughby feared that someday, some reporters would want to write a profile of *him*. This sort of publicity was anathema to most consultants, doubly so to Willoughby, given his peculiar practice of playing—and profiting from—both sides of a controversy. His business practice was familiar to insiders (by now, most of them had caught on to the meaning of Janus); they knew how the game was played, how all consultants fudged their findings to the needs of their clients. But splashing his M.O. in headlines might damage his brand, might raise questions all too explicitly about the value of his work: if the consultant didn't believe in his conclusions, some might ask, why should the client—and why should the officials and lawmakers that the client was trying to influence? It was best in this business, Willoughby learned long ago, to keep a low profile.

But Willoughby knew one reporter who might be worth approaching with a deflective slant on the Chinese spy story—Natalie Gold, the sole writer, researcher, editor, and publisher of an online newsletter called *The Gold Mine*. It was strictly an insider's news sheet, limited to five thousand password-protected subscribers, who each paid $2,500 a year for the privilege of reading Gold's scoops, insights, and analyses about the hot flashes and long-term trends in the subterranean realms of the American military and intelligence agencies—often esoteric but, to its elite readers, essential.

Willoughby was one of those subscribers, and he'd earned back the annual fee, several times over, from the information he gleaned, inferred, and exploited to propose lucrative projects a step or two ahead of the competition. He'd once met Natalie Gold, nearly a year ago, at a party. She chatted him up, eager to learn more about his background and his techniques. He evaded her questions, leery of her intentions; she was a reporter, after all. But now he needed a reporter, and Gold would be better than most: more thorough, more knowledgeable, and writing for a more exclusive readership—precisely the upper-echelon officials and bureaucrats that Willoughby needed in order to allay the suspicions surrounding Mandelbaum and, by extension, himself.

He emailed Gold, suggesting a lunch, and, after a couple of back-and-forth missives, they agreed to meet the next day, at noon, in a restaurant a couple blocks north of Willoughby's office. He arrived, as usual, a few minutes early. At 12:00 precisely, Gold blew through the door and glided toward his table, as if propelled by a fine-tuned engine or a breeze-swept sail.

"Serge, I need to visit this part of town more often," she said, talking at a fast, smooth clip, in a familiar, balmy tone even before sitting down. "I was a little early, so I dropped in at that used bookstore across DuPont Circle—my God, what a treasure trove, look at this." She pulled out a large, pristine, linen-bound edition of

Harold Feinstein's *Retrospective*. "I've been trying to find a good copy for years, and there it was, just sitting on the counter. Do you know Feinstein? Say what you will about Friedlander, Eggleston, Meyerowitz, even *Robert Frank*"—she whispered the name as if invoking a god, then revved back to her jet stream speed—"I believe Feinstein is the true poet among urban street photographers, I don't care what anybody says. Listen," she went on, not missing a beat, "I have to pee, I'll be right back."

Willoughby sat in a daze, unsure which spark of her fireball entrance he found most beguiling. First, she turned out to be a knockout, and he wasn't expecting that. At the party where he'd met her, she'd worn the standard-issue Washington woman's red power dress with her hair knotted up. Now, for their lunch, she was decked out in a pleated chiffon skirt, a sheer sleeveless blouse draped with an explosively colored silk scarf, her hair raven, shoulder-length, and frizzy, perfectly coiffed except for one tangled strand that kept tumbling in front of her right eye (it was hard to tell whether this was part of the look or a vestige of an underlying dishevelment), and—the pièce de résistance—black horn-rimmed glasses, propped by flame-red titanium stems, all fashionably elegant and fearsomely intellectual. Willoughby was smitten.

Then there was the book that she'd pulled out of her bag. Was this a karmic coincidence—were the two of them destined to while away the next few hours, exploring the many passions that they doubtlessly shared—or did she *know* that he owned *two* Harold Feinstein prints, which held pride of place on his living room wall? Had she scoped him out, like the object of a reconnaissance mission? He wondered if she'd really bought the book on the way to lunch, or if she'd acquired it much earlier, setting it aside for just this moment. He looked inside the shopping bag and spied a receipt, itemizing $300 for one book (presumably the Feinstein, a reasonable price, given the market for such a rarity) and $4 for another. He felt around for the other book and found a thin paperback. It was *Selected Poems* by W.H. Auden, the same Faber and Faber edition that he'd bought on Charing Cross Road decades ago, during his college years, on a spring break trip, his first ever overseas voyage, to London.

Either this meeting was a twist of fate, the likes of which unfold only in cornball movies, or Natalie Gold was quite the operator. Was this how she eked information from well-placed sources: find their soft spot and massage it relentlessly? But Willoughby was the one who'd called the meeting—*he* had a plan to play *her*. Now, it seemed, she had a plan to play him, too, but what was her game?

She returned to the table. Willoughby decided to stay mum on his discoveries and musings. The fact that he said nothing about his two Feinstein prints would tip her off that he saw through her elaborate ploy and wasn't playing along (though a small part of Willoughby, the few atoms that had survived his soul-soaking cynicism, stoked the hope, however remote, that her penchant for Feinstein and Auden was genuine). She sat there, silent, uncharacteristically so, judging from her walk-on just minutes before, possibly waiting for Willoughby to follow her cue. When he didn't, she called over a waiter to take their orders, then moved on to business. "So, Serge," she said finally, "why did you call me?"

Willoughby recited the pitch that he'd rehearsed beforehand. The NSA, he told her in hushed tones, was involved in a misbegotten, potentially destructive operation tracking an alleged ring of Chinese spies who were phoning coded messages to a hardware store in suburban Maryland. The thing is, he went on, regular customers were calling in actual orders, and the FBI was placing these innocent citizens under harsh surveillance. He knew a couple of people who'd been arrested for making completely innocuous calls. It was a scandal; it was going to backfire, do damage to real counterintelligence ops.

Gold seemed intrigued, took a few notes, asked a few follow-up questions (to which Willoughby mustered a few vague replies). They ate their meals, making small talk (about the weather, the stock market, the crazy Congress). Then she got up, thanked him, and said she'd be in touch.

At 9:00 that night, the Signal app buzzed on Willoughby's cell phone. He picked it up. It was Gold.

"Listen, Serge," she began, not even saying hello. "That NSA operation is the real deal. The phone number the spies are calling is hooked up to an unlisted answering machine that's used only by the spies. It's not connected to the hardware store's public line, so no real customers would call it. This means that your two friends—I take it Wolf Mandelbaum is one of them—either dialed a wrong number or they're spies, and I doubt the FBI would have arrested them if what they said indicated they'd dialed a wrong number."

Willoughby was impressed that Gold had found out so much so quickly, but he also sensed danger signs flashing. "How do you know about Wolf Mandelbaum?" he asked. He hadn't mentioned that name at the lunch.

"What do you think I do for a living?" she replied. "Do you think you come to me with a story and I don't check it with other sources and follow the facts where they lead?"

"Look, Natalie," he said. "There was a party at Wolf's that night. He might not have been the one who called the number."

"Do you know something you're not telling me?" Gold asked. Willoughby stayed silent. Five seconds passed. "Holy shit, Serge! Did *you* make that call, as some sort of *prank*?"

Christ, she's fast, Willoughby thought. He was so stunned, his throat jammed, he was physically unable to laugh away the notion or to say anything.

"Oh, *man!*" she said, then heaved the loudest, most exasperated sigh that he'd ever heard. "I'm coming over."

"Wait, my address—" he began.

"I think you know I know where you live," she said, at once amused and condescending, then hung up.

Twenty minutes later, she rang his doorbell, having presumably eluded or sweet-talked the doorman seven stories below. Willoughby let her in. She'd toned down her style from earlier that day: her hair was more naturally frizzy, the haute couture outfit replaced by slacks and a loose-fitting sweater, both black. She floated through the foyer into the living room, as if she'd mapped out the floor plan in advance (had she?), and sat down on his favorite chair, a French Art Deco antique, passing the two Feinstein prints on her way and barely giving them a glance. (So much for Willoughby's moony half hope that some shared aesthetic taste had fated them to meet.) Willoughby sat opposite her on a matching leather sofa.

"Here's the thing," Gold began. "My article reporting the arrest of Wolf Mandelbaum goes up online in the next couple of minutes."

"You couldn't have waited a little?" Willoughby moaned.

"No," she answered. "The *Times* was on my tail, and my customers don't pay me for day-old bread. However," she added, "I did *not* report that the FBI has detained or flipped a few Chinese nationals. I didn't even mention the phone at the hardware store, because I don't blow ongoing intel operations. Even about Mandelbaum, I wrote that he was being *questioned* about *connections* to Chinese intelligence.

"So, here's what's going to happen," she went on, as if reading Willoughby his rights. "Some spymaster in Beijing will read my story about Mandelbaum. One possibility: he'll say, 'Who the fuck is Wolf Mandelbaum?' Which means your friend isn't a spy and he'll probably be let go. But then the Feds will start wondering who *did* make that phone call from his house that night, and they might start thinking *you're* the Chinese spy." She paused. "*Are* you a Chinese spy, Serge?"

"Seriously?" Willoughby asked, in a more nervous tone than he meant to convey.

"The other possibility," Gold continued, "is the reader in Beijing will say, 'Holy shit, the Americans have arrested one of our top spies in Washington,' and his bosses in the defense ministry will make some crazy aggressive moves in the Taiwan Strait or the South China Sea. In sum," she concluded, "thanks to your cockamamie stunt at Mandelbaum's, either you're going to be in trouble or the whole world is going to be in trouble."

"But wait," Willoughby said. "Why do you think there's the slightest chance that's going to happen? Why do you think Mandelbaum *is* a spy? The only evidence he *might* be is the phone call, and he didn't make that call."

"I've only scratched the surface of this so far," Gold said, "but apparently, there's other evidence of contacts between Mandelbaum and Chinese officials here in Washington and in New York. In other words, Serge, you might have framed a guilty man."

Willoughby gulped.

Anyway," she went on, "if Mandelbaum is let off the hook and you take his place, that's your problem. But if he isn't and the hounds of war start howling in Asia Pacific, then you and I will have to work together to keep them at bay, nip the battle in the bud, save the planet." She said all this seemingly without irony.

Willoughby laughed. "The two of us are going to save the world?" he asked with heaps of sarcasm.

"Sure," she replied. "Why do *you* get up and go to work every morning? What do you see as the *purpose* of your life?"

Willoughby felt a pall of dread enveloping his entire being, not just for the deadly catastrophe that his act of spite might soon spring upon all of humanity but also for the piercing wound of Natalie Gold's simple question and its exposure of the hollowness at his core, his betrayal of all the talent and privilege that life had bestowed upon him to pursue a career of clever political gamesmanship, which had rewarded him with money and leisure, but left him bereft of—what was Gold's eyebrow-arched word?—*purpose*.

Then again, Natalie Gold wasn't exactly some AIDS nurse or Peace Corps volunteer. Where did *she* come off slamming *him* for a decrepit moral sense?

"Get some rest," Gold said, rising from the chair. "Whichever way this thing goes, you've got a lot of work to do tomorrow."

Willoughby followed and opened the door to let her out.

One step into the hallway, she turned and faced him. "By the way, Serge," she said in a voice softer than any he'd heard from her all evening, "I *did* notice the two Feinstein prints. They're wonderful, among his best, I think. Your taste is exquisite." She low-beamed him a Mona Lisa smile, turned away, and sauntered toward the elevator.

Willoughby shut the door, discombobulated. What was *that* about? Was she outlining a plausible scenario or playing another mind game? And what about her exit line and that smile? Was she a Feinstein fan after all? Willoughby felt light-headed, dazed to the point of dizzy, and, for the first time in weeks, very horny.

CHAPTER 3

The next morning, at just past 8:00, the phone rang. It was Natalie Gold. "It's happening. Turn on the BBC." Then she hung up.

Willoughby did as he was told. The dulcet-toned newscaster was reciting a gale storm of world-altering news.

Chinese jet fighters were buzzing an American aircraft carrier in the South China Sea.

Hundreds of Chinese troops were gathering at the docks along the Taiwan Strait, apparently to board a flotilla of merchant marine ships.

Meanwhile, an American reconnaissance satellite perched overhead blacked out, possibly the result of an attack by a Chinese rocket or perhaps simply a battery failure, as had occurred with an identical satellite a few months earlier.

In any case, two more US aircraft carriers were steaming to the region, while American troops in Guam, Okinawa, and Australia were placed on high alert.

The phone rang again. It was Isaiah "Ike" Douglass, an old friend of Willoughby's, a retired Army colonel, and, for the past year, special assistant to the secretary of defense—not a government official but a consultant, an unusual type, who worked for just one client.

"I assume you're following the news," Douglass said.

"Of course," Willoughby replied, not letting on that he'd been doing so for not quite two minutes.

"This is a major escalation from the ChiComm's usual pattern of cage rattling," Douglass said, invoking the Cold War-era's abbreviation for Chinese Communist. "I wanted to let you know that the secretary and the Joint Chiefs are crafting a response, and it's modeled very much after your study."

"My study?"

"Yes, the study you did for Indo-Pacific Command, *An Escalation-Dominance Strategy for a US–China Conflict.*"

"I wrote that study three years ago," Willoughby objected, still uneasily digesting the news that not only had his phone prank at Mandelbaum's provoked what was shaping up to be a major war, but a study he'd once written (and barely remembered) was about to be adopted as the official US war plan.

"Not to worry," Douglass said. "The ops guys are plugging in new numbers. But pretty much everyone has signed off on your concept."

Willoughby was shaken fully awake now, memories of this study flooding his brain cells. It was one of his very few projects in military *operations*, a genre that he tended to avoid. He was a *procurement* man, analyzing which weapons to buy or not to buy. Procurement was a straightforward business: there were clear data, or at least a clear range of estimates, on costs and benefits (the estimates might be inaccurate, but that wasn't his problem—the client supplied them with the assignment), whereas there were too many imponderables in warfare. More to the point, studies on procurement were, comfortably, of little consequence—a wrongheaded conclusion might result in a waste of money—but a poorly wrought war plan could sow the downfall of a nation and kill thousands of civilians, even millions if the war wildly escalated. Simply put, Willoughby didn't want the responsibility.

He'd been persuaded to do the study because the Air Force and the Navy were updating their joint operations plan for war with the People's Republic of China. It was a pretty routine task, scenario-writing straight out of Game Theory 101 (what is our best move at each stage of the conflict, assuming the enemy makes his best move), requiring no special expertise on Chinese history, politics, or culture. And like all Pentagon-commissioned studies of this sort, it concluded—its premises were designed to make it conclude—that the US would win the war.

But Willoughby now remembered that, around the same time, in the Janus Corporation tradition, he also wrote a study reaching the exact opposite conclusion: that the American military would emerge from this war in terrible shape. The top officers of the Marine Corps had looked at the study he'd done for the Air Force and the Navy, saw that one phase of its scenario envisioned Marines making an amphibious landing along the coast of mainland China, and knew full well that, in real life, this would result in a rout, a total bloodbath.

So they recruited Willoughby (everyone had long understood the drill) to reexamine the data from (to put it delicately) "an alternative angle." He gave the resulting paper exactly the same title as the earlier, more gung-ho study—*An Escalation-Dominance Strategy for a US–China Conflict*—but with three words tacked on top: "*The Risks of.*"

"Ike," Willoughby asked, "did you, or anyone else over there, happen to read the study I did on the same topic for the Marines?"

"No, why would anybody do that?" Douglass replied, with the contempt that most Army officers harbored for the Marines (and vice versa).

"Well, it came to a *very* different conclusion," Willoughby said, his voice rising slightly, "a conclusion so different that it might make *anybody* a bit *leery* about going to war."

Douglass was silent.

"Listen, Ike, you owe me a very big favor, and I'm calling it in now. I need to have a meeting with the secretary—it shouldn't take more than ten minutes—and I need to have it today."

Willoughby wasn't exaggerating about the favor he was owed. Back at the height of the Iraq War, when roadside bombs were killing American troops every day, practically every hour, Douglass was a mid-level officer in the Pentagon, urging his superiors to buy a new sturdy lightweight troop carrier called the MRAP (Mine-Resistant, Ambush-Protective) vehicle, but the Army's top brass were against the idea. They were looking beyond the present conflict, which they viewed as a distraction—a "small war"—and preferred to invest their money in things like heavy tanks, missiles, and artillery rockets for the *big* war ahead. Douglass was apoplectic: his fellow soldiers were fighting, killing, and dying in a war *right now*. He took his gripes, behind the scenes, to a few Pentagon civilians, who directed him to the Janus Corporation. Willoughby remembered their first phone call, this hardened combat veteran reduced to the edge of tears, practically begging him to do a study that might validate the MRAP. Willoughby drew up a contract and did the work, concluding that MRAPs would in fact save the lives of hundreds, maybe thousands of American troops at a price that, though high, was much cheaper than other ways of saving lives on the battlefield.

As it happened, he did not do the contrary study. The Army's in-house analysts wrote their own rebuttal of Willoughby's work, and the product was less than compelling. The Janus study made its way to senior officials in the Pentagon and to a few key senators, who, together, added an extraordinary 16 billion dollars to the budget for accelerated production of MRAPs. The Army brass never forgave Douglass for his impertinence; he was transferred to clerical jobs at cold, distant bases and repeatedly denied promotion. Finally, he retired, gave speeches, and wrote articles about the Pentagon's bureaucratic maladies. The current secretary of defense heard one of his speeches shortly after his Senate confirmation, talked with Douglass afterward at length, and hired him as his right-hand reality checker. So, in a roundabout way, Willoughby was responsible for Douglass' new, more satisfying, and much more powerful phase of his career. But the key thing, Douglass had stressed many times, was that, had it not been for Willoughby's study, a lot of his comrades in arms, some of them close friends, would have died.

"I owe you a very big favor," Douglass told him at the time. "Call it in whenever you like."

Willoughby always felt a bit churlish about the offer. If he had followed his usual practice, if the brass had asked the Janus Corporation to do a study concluding that the MRAP was a waste of money, he would have done it for the sake of doubling his fee. His rebuttal would have been more persuasive than the Army's, possibly more persuasive than his own original study; as a result, more MRAPs might not have been purchased and more American soldiers might have died. In retrospect, Willoughby was glad that he hadn't worked the customary Janus magic; he was glad that things worked out the way they did (he wasn't a monster, after all). But it was only by chance that he had helped save all those lives and earned Ike Douglass' gratitude.

Still, a favor was a favor, and now Willoughby was calling it in.

Douglass honored it without hesitation. "The secretary is in a meeting at the White House now," he replied, "but he's testifying before the House Armed Services Committee at thirteen hundred hours. That's one o'clock this afternoon."

"Yes, I know it's one o'clock this afternoon," Willoughby sighed, rolling his eyes. "I know how to speak military time."

"Come to the hearing," Douglass said. "I'll make sure you have a seat in the secretary's limo back to the Pentagon afterward."

Willoughby hung up the phone. He took a gulp of the coffee that he'd poured before the phone calls from Gold and Douglass, but it had gone cold and he shoved the cup aside. He sighed, got up out of his chair, and walked around his apartment a few times, thinking.

He needed to brief the secretary and, if possible, the military chiefs on *both* of his China-war studies. He'd never briefed both papers on a topic—the emblematic two faces of a Janus Corporation product—to the same audience. But if the Pentagon's top officials were going to war on the assurances offered by his first study, and if the war escalated notch by notch to the highest, most destructive level (Willoughby recalled that the final move of his "escalation-dominance" scenario involved launching a small volley of nuclear missiles), then he had to let them in on the results of his second study.

To do this, he had to bring both studies up to date. Douglass had said the ops officers had plugged new numbers into his old study. If his conversation with the secretary was to pack a punch, Willoughby might have to plug in new numbers too. He didn't have time to do the research, but he knew someone who'd already done it: Vijay Gupta, the job applicant he'd interviewed the day before—the author of, among other mind-numbing but doubtlessly pertinent studies, *A Data Compendium on Worldwide Air and Maritime Forces.*

He phoned Gupta, who answered on the second ring.

"Vijay Gupta? This is Serge Willoughby. Do you want that job?" he asked

"Sure," Gupta answered after a pause that lasted a little too long.

"It's yours," Willoughby said. "Meet me at my office in an hour."

Willoughby arrived a half hour before then. He'd asked Donna Cappella to pull the two studies out of his safe and place them on his desk. He went into his office, sat down, and looked them over. Attached to each hefty document was a three-page summary of the oral briefing that he had delivered to the clients. To refresh his memory, he read the briefings and then skimmed the full studies.

Given what was going on now halfway around the world, they reeked of an appallingly casual confidence.

Donna Capella appeared in his doorway. "Are we about to go to war?" she asked nervously. "Isn't Washington DC 'ground zero' for an enemy nuclear attack? Should I get out of town, maybe visit my sister in Minnesota?"

Willoughby was struck. Donna Cappella was as imperturbable a soul as he'd ever met. If she was frazzled by the world's events, then the population as a whole must be in a panic.

"Don't buy any plane tickets just yet," Willoughby replied. "Believe it or not, I'm working on getting us all out of danger."

Donna Cappella emitted a short, steely laugh, as if his assurance was a sick joke—which, Willoughby had to admit to himself, it probably was.

Just then, Gupta entered the front door to the office. He was on time. Willoughby gave him the three-page summaries. "I want you to read these briefings and revise them with up-to-date numbers."

Gupta looked down at the sheets and widened his eyes. "But these are classified—they're stamped 'secret,'" he exclaimed, in a bit of shock. "I don't have a security clearance."

"Don't worry. You've met Donna Cappella," Willoughby calmly assured him, nodding in her direction. "Give her your full name, address, date of birth, place of birth, and Social Security number. She'll phone our contact in the Pentagon's public affairs office, and you'll get an *interim* Secret clearance right away."

"Really? It's that simple?" Gupta asked.

Willoughby waved away his concerns. "Secret doesn't mean squat," he said brusquely. "If you were a Chinese spy and you gave your handlers every Pentagon document stamped Secret, they wouldn't learn a damn thing. Believe me, the numbers in this briefing are no more sensitive than the numbers in your *Data Compendium*, except that your numbers are more detailed and more current. I need you to take the numbers in my briefings, which were written three years ago, and substitute the numbers from your monograph. I have to go to the Hill in a few minutes. Text me the revisions by, let's say, one-thirty. OK?"

Willoughby returned to his office, shut the door, and called Giles Molloy, who picked up the phone promptly.

"Giles, sorry I didn't call you back yesterday—things have been hectic," Willoughby began. "Have you heard anything new about Wolf?"

"No, except I see that Natalie Gold confirms what I told you about his arrest," Molloy said.

"Do you subscribe to her newsletter?" Willoughby asked, a bit surprised.

"Noooooo. Too rich for my blood. But I have friends who have friends who read me the good parts over the telephone. Have you ever met her?"

"Just a couple times," Willoughby said, evasively.

"Watch yourself very carefully if she ever asks you questions. She extracts information from sources so deftly, they don't realize what they're giving her. She seems to know almost everything from the get-go, so people let her in on some minor detail—yeah, it's classified, but you know, there's classified and there's *classified*. Then it turns out that the minor detail was just what she needed to fill in the last blank for the *really* secret scoop she'd been piecing together."

Willoughby wondered if she had done that at some point with Molloy, which led him to wonder if she was doing it now with *him*. "Do you believe Wolf Mandelbaum is a Chinese spy?"

"Beats me. He did keep harping on about the Russian threat long after the rest of this town shifted to the Chinese peril. Then again, maybe he was just prescient."

Willoughby had called with the intention of telling his old mentor about the prank phone call and asking for advice on what to do. Molloy had taught him a lot of the tricks of the trade, along with the basic premise that much of what propelled this town's passions was a joke. He had also introduced Willoughby to Mandelbaum.

"Wolf is a legend—he'll be invaluable for contacts," Molloy had told him just days after the Janus Corporation's launch. "Serge is a huge talent—he'll keep you on your toes," he had told Mandelbaum around the same time.

The meeting happened, and before too long Willoughby was a fixture at the Mandelbaum home for various events. As an isolated memory, Willoughby looked back fondly on that time of scintillating brunches and dinners. He felt the frisson of membership in an elite circle, Wolf holding court on politics, philosophy, culture, or culinary delicacies while uncorking another fine Bordeaux, the small coterie of invited guests—most of them colleagues, some of them Wolf's employees—laughing and nodding at the wisdom of their host, who would allow Serge an occasional say, which prompted another round of laughter and nods, less hearty but still gratifying.

At one of these lunches, just the three of them, Mandelbaum suggested that Willoughby come work for him, or, as he put it, come work *with* him—not just an invitation, but a suggestion of peer status, which the young novice took as license to comment critically on the old master's work, as a respected colleague might do. Around that time, while digging into the studies more deeply, looking up the footnotes, checking the math, Willoughby had discovered Mandelbaum's many mistakes. So he pointed out a few of them, thinking that he'd be thanked and further rewarded for his diligence. Instead, the master gradually cut the upstart off, invited him to fewer and fewer soirées, and stopped recommending him to prospective clients altogether. Molloy, who remained a mentor through this chapter of his life, was a contemporary and friend of Mandelbaum's, so Willoughby didn't complain about the slight, though Molloy noticed it and offered no rebuttal—instead, nodded sadly—on the one occasion when Willoughby recited the egregious flaws in a particular Mandelbaum study.

So, Willoughby now reflected, Molloy knew all about his checkered history with Mandelbaum and would understand an outburst of bitterness. Nonetheless, *pranking* the man, pranking any fellow consultants, would be seen as crossing several bridges too far. And a prank that wound up getting a fellow consultant in trouble with the law might be seen as unforgivable.

He was too ashamed to tell Molloy what he had done. "Keep me posted if you hear anything," Willoughby said softly, and, ashamed that he felt so ashamed, he hung up.

The House hearing didn't begin for another hour, so Willoughby walked the three miles to Capitol Hill, outlining in his head the ten-minute pitch that he hoped to deliver to the secretary of defense. He didn't relish the prospect of witnessing a House hearing. The whole scene brought back too many bad memories. In the forty years since he'd worked on the Hill, he could count maybe a dozen times when he visited some legislator's office or attended a congressionally sponsored event, and even then, only because there had been some obligation to do so.

Walking around Washington DC, especially the expanse between DuPont Circle and the Capitol, made Willoughby feel like a relic. So much had changed since he arrived. Passing certain corners, he could almost see the shadows of old haunts—bookshops, record stores, and movie theaters, now transmogrified into bank branches, juice cafes, and workout palaces, if not torn down entirely. Other changes simply astonished him. Whole blocks that had once been blighted slums, working-class neighborhoods razed in the riots of '68, then left to rot, were now revived, the outgrowth of cash flooding the capital over a stream of decades—mainly on the rising tides of lobbying firms, defense contractors, spy-software labs, and consultancies like his—transforming the fringes of downtown DC into a booming city center of luxury condos, office buildings, fine restaurants, and a convention complex, though nearly all of them crammed into soul-crushing demi-towers of glass and concrete.

He took a detour, turning south, then headed east again when he reached the Washington Mall, one of the rare untrammeled stretches of the old city, its rolling meadows cupping the treasures of the National Archive, the National Gallery, and the monuments and memorials in the distance. Finally, he approached the great structure of the Capitol—"The People's House," some still called it without irony—and he felt a tingle of awe, despite himself. Such a grand spectacle: the neo-classical dome and pillars, the finely sculpted grounds with their curved walkways and bronze lamps, the twigs and branches from the flanking shrubbery swaying in a rhythm of challenge and contentment—this was holy ground, democracy's brightest glimmerings. But then his brief reverie shattered into shards, overtaken by a sudden remembrance of the stark contrast between the architectural wonderment and the all-too-human reality—a palace of glorious hopes, wasted on the tawdry mediocrities who presently prowled its corridors.

Turning a block past the Capitol's southern corner, he sighed for a moment before heading into the Rayburn House Office Building, where he flashed his ID, cleared the metal detector, climbed the spiral staircase to the second floor, and, with a discomfiting tinge of regret, entered room 2118, the spare but splendid main hearing room of the committee for which he once worked. He took a seat near the back, off to the side, and watched the lawmakers entering the chamber and settling into their chairs on the dais. He stared with special interest at the young staff members filling the rows behind their bosses, their briefcases bulging with budget books, talking point sheets, and other thick documents. He wondered what was swirling through their energetic minds, what ideals or ambitions animated their fervor, whether they harbored the same illusions that had driven him back when he held their positions. He studied their faces and body language, imagining which of them would soon snap out of the dream and which would stay entombed in a perpetual stupor.

He heard muffled voices behind him, turned, and saw his friend Ike Douglass entering the chamber, hoisting a big satchel, followed by his boss, the secretary of defense, James Weed Portis. The two formed an odd couple: Douglass, a tall, burly African-American man who spoke in a baritone and looked a lot like Frederick Douglass, whom he claimed as a distant relative (though he once confessed to Willoughby that the connection was probably family mythology); Portis, a short, pale New Englander with slicked back white hair and a reedy voice. Almost a decade older than Willoughby, Portis harked back to cabinet secretaries of the Cold War era: corporate chieftains from elite families—in Portis's case, an investment banker bred in

Maine and schooled at Harvard—who pursued America's global interests without strain or doubt because those interests meshed so seamlessly with their own. He dressed old-school too: dark blue pinstriped suit, Turnbull & Asser shirt, pocket square handkerchief, gold tie pin and cufflinks.

As with many patrician men in public life, Portis' mild manner was deceptive. Once, at a reception, Willoughby saw him deflate a highly regarded think tank scholar with such brutal efficiency, responding to some obtuse cliché by narrowing his eyes to a steely glint and muttering an admonishment so quiet yet stern ("You would be well-advised not to publish that," were the words he chiseled in the surrounding air), that even Willoughby—who wasn't part of the conversation, but merely observed it from a few feet away—felt the hairs rise on the back of his neck. Willoughby had met Portis a few times. Their conversations were cordial, but he was frankly terrified of the man. Douglass once told him that those who thought Portis was their friend called him Jim, while those who really were friends called him Weed. Willoughby called him Mr. Secretary.

The committee chairman pounded the gavel, and brought the hearing to order. Struggling to stay awake through the opening remarks, Willoughby realized that this was a routine hearing on the defense budget—odd, he thought, given what was going on in the world, but he was long past trying to make sense of Congress. When the chairman finished, the ranking minority member read his own opening remarks. These forgettable bits of oratory, together, consumed twenty minutes. The floor was then turned over to Portis, who thanked the members for convening the hearing, said that he would skip reading his written testimony and instead submit it for the record, given his need to return to the Pentagon sooner than originally scheduled in order to deal with the China crisis, but noted that he had agreed to sit for one five-minute round of questions from each of the members.

At this point, the chairman consumed another five minutes uttering clichés about the vast challenges facing the nation, then asked Portis, "Do you believe in the proposition that the United

States must fully fund the modernization of all three legs of the strategic triad?"

He was referring to the three types of weapons systems—the land-based intercontinental ballistic missiles, the submarine-launched ballistic missiles, and the heavy bombers—that could fire nuclear warheads or drop nuclear bombs on targets halfway around the world. It had long been an all-but-unquestioned mantra, even back in Willoughby's time on the Hill, that the nation needed all three means of performing this cataclysmic mission. The notion now seemed elevated to an article of faith, the triad regarded with the same trembling veneration that Catholics devoted to the Holy Trinity of the Father, the Son, and the Holy Ghost.

"I believe in the necessity of a safe, secure, and reliable nuclear deterrent that is credible to our adversaries and reassuring to our allies," Portis replied.

The exchange really was like a prayer-book catechism, though Willoughby knew that Douglass wasn't a true believer (the Army no longer possessed nuclear weapons, and never had any long-range nuclear missiles, so most Army generals had little interest in them), and he suspected that, deep down, Portis wasn't either.

The ranking minority member asked if our troops were capable of meeting America's obligations under Article 5 of the NATO treaty, which committed member states to consider an attack on any one of them as an attack on them all.

Portis replied, "American armed forces are indeed *fully* ready." Another scripted shibboleth.

As the more junior legislators were called upon to pose for their C-Span moments, the questions turned bizarre. A congressman from Texas wanted to know if the troops returning from the Middle East might be redeployed to his home state's base at Fort Bliss. "There's plenty of room for y'all," he assured the secretary, though added, "We *would* need larger appropriations for construction of family housing."

A congresswoman from California brought up the crisis in the Taiwan Strait (*Finally!* Willoughby thought), but only to ask if it might affect the supply chain for microchips used in gaming consoles manufactured in her district. A congressman from Arizona inquired about the status of a research and development project, which he'd introduced as an amendment the previous year, on irritable bowel syndrome ("the dark, shameful malady that clogs the fighting spirit of our servicemen and women more than many know," he intoned).

Willoughby hadn't watched a congressional hearing for a long time, and now he remembered why. The institution had taken a ghastly tumble since his time. The debates may have been phony in his days on the Hill, but at least there were debates. Then again, maybe the good old days were worse; maybe the new era of shallow dogma and naked self-interest was better. There was a lack of pretense, a shameless transparency that, in a certain mood, he might have found refreshing. But at the moment, he was merely dispirited.

He felt the cell phone vibrating in his pocket. He took it out and looked at the screen. It was his new hire, Vijay Gupta, texting the revised numbers for his study, with the header, "Call me! Urgent!" Willoughby crept out of the hearing room into the hallway to make the call. Gupta picked up on the first ring.

"Thanks for the numbers," Willoughby said. "What's urgent?"

"Oh, you're welcome," Gupta replied. "I was reading the summaries for both reports, and, well, they come to diametrically opposite conclusions."

"Yes, I'm aware of that," Willoughby said dryly. Molloy clearly hadn't filled the kid in on the nature of the firm.

"Would you like me to analyze the strengths and weaknesses of each?" Gupta earnestly asked.

"No, I think I've got that under control," Willoughby replied.

"There *is* one thing that you may not know, but should," Gupta said with a welcome firmness that Willoughby hadn't previously heard in his voice.

"Yes?"

"In the version you wrote for the Air Force and the Navy," Gupta began, "you assumed, toward the end, that we can disrupt a Chinese nuclear response by launching a cyberattack on their command and control systems. Well, when I was writing *The Influence of Cyber Technologies on the Strategic Nuclear Balance*, I

51

originally made the same assumption. But then I had an interesting conversation with a very senior officer from Cyber Command who happened to be visiting the RAND campus, and he told me this assumption might be—in fact, probably is—fallacious."

"Go on," Willoughby said, suddenly riveted after his attention had begun to wander during Gupta's throat-clearing preamble.

"He told me that Cyber Command did try to block two Chinese ICBM test launches, and the tactic seemed to work: the missiles fizzled on the launch pad," Gupta said. "But then it tried for a third time and a fourth time, and both of those missiles blasted off without a hitch. So, nobody knows whether we can really do this. Maybe the cyberattack *did* block the first two tests, and maybe the Chinese detected the attack and developed a work-around for the next two tests. Or maybe it was all a coincidence. Maybe the first two tests failed for reasons having nothing to do with what we tried to do."

"That's very helpful, Gupta," Willoughby said. This could be another bullet point in his case that going to war with China—especially in the way suggested by his own study on how to go to war with China—would be riskier than Portis and the generals seemed to think.

When Willoughby returned to the chamber, the hearing was wrapping up.

"We thank you for your time, Mr. Secretary," the chairman was saying. "And if you could get back to us with the precise figures on cost overruns in the maintenance accounts for commissaries at our military bases in South Asia, I would appreciate it."

As Portis rose to leave, Douglass cocked his eyebrow at Willoughby and motioned for him to follow. The three of them, along with a couple of security officers, walked very quickly out the door, down the stairway, out of the building, and into an awaiting limousine. Portis and Douglass settled into the soft leather cushion in the back seat. Willoughby made himself as comfortable as possible (which wasn't very) on the small round pull-down seat facing them.

"Those *motherfuckers!*" Portis roared, once the door was closed.

"They're *cocksuckers!*" Douglass chimed in.

"Ike, is there any way I can cancel every *goddamned* military contract in every *fucking* district of every *son of a bitch* on that whole *shit-for-brains* committee?" Portis asked.

"I'm afraid not, sir," Douglass replied.

Willoughby was startled. He was no prude when it came to profanity and could let loose streams of it on fitting occasions, but he'd never heard anything quite like this. Douglass had once told him that, unlike most defense secretaries, who prepare for congressional hearings by reciting polite responses to likely questions, Portis treated his rehearsals as scream-therapy sessions, barking the fiercest, foulest obscenities he could muster, to vent the anger and frustration out of his system, so that he could come off as calm and respectful in his actual testimony. Willoughby suspected that the morning meeting in the White House had preempted Portis's cathartic rant ritual, so he must have been holding in the rage as the annoyances of the hearing intensified, and now he was erupting in a bender of fury, with his assistant joining in, as assistants do.

Portis looked at Willoughby, as if nothing unusual had just happened, and said, with no special intonation, "Ike tells me you want to say a few words about the China crisis."

"Yes, Mr. Secretary, thank you for agreeing to see me on such short notice," Willoughby began. "I'm told that the war plan, which you and the chiefs are about to endorse, is based on a study that I wrote for the Air Force and Navy a few years ago, which came to quite optimistic conclusions. I think you and the chiefs need to know that, around the same time, I wrote a study for the Marine Corps— a much less widely read report, I'm told—which looked at the problem from a more cautionary perspective."

Willoughby felt vaguely ashamed of his opening lines, which, he knew the moment he spoke them, reeked of an unseemly evasiveness. He looked over to Douglass for a comforting gesture, but his friend was riveted to his phone, frantically typing out a text message.

"Which of the two studies did you believe in?" Portis asked, a scowl forming.

"Well, that would depend on the analytic assumptions," Willoughby replied, again inadequately.

"Yes, Ike has told me about your *flexible methodology*," Portis said, the scowl now fully formed. "I must say, it strikes me that you're running a *racket*." That steely glint flashed in the secretary's eyes, and Willoughby felt not only the hairs rise on the back of his neck but a thick tremor rolling up his spine.

"Then again," Portis grumbled, "this whole fucking town is one big racket. I've worked my entire adult life on Wall Street, where the only goal is to make money. Some people have a problem with that, but we don't make any bones about it, and, as long as we abide by lawful regulations and our fiduciary responsibilities, we're doing the jobs that we say we set out to do. I had the naïve impression when I took *this* goddamned job that I'd be working with people whose goal was to protect and promote the security of the United States of America and its allies. It turns out that here too, everybody's just in it for themselves, but, unlike the colleagues in my old world, they're not *supposed* to be—so they're just *fucking things up*."

By this time, the limo was pulling into the Pentagon driveway. "Ike has lined up an audience to hear your briefing," Portis said. "What time does it begin, Ike?"

"Fifteen hundred hours, sir," Douglass replied.

"Speak the King's English, for chrissakes," Portis shot back, only a little playfully.

"Three o'clock PM, sir," he clarified.

That was in five minutes.

"Can I ask a question that hasn't been addressed in the news stories I've seen?" Willoughby asked. "Why are the Chinese doing what they're doing? What set them off? What's the *cause* of this war, if we're about to start fighting one?"

Portis and Douglass exchanged a furtive glance, then Douglass looked down as Portis stared at Willoughby with that glint in his eyes again. "We can't talk about that just now," he said softly but piercingly.

Did Willoughby's call from Mandelbaum's phone really set this off? *Was* Mandelbaum a spy? And how much did Portis and Douglass know about what happened at the party that night? Willoughby felt a wavelet of dread coming on.

CHAPTER 4

The briefing took place in the spacious, oak-trimmed office of the secretary of defense on the third floor of the Pentagon's innermost E-Ring. Willoughby had been there several times over the years and found it either majestic or comical, depending on its occupant. This time, the first time he'd been there since Portis was sworn in, its grandeur or grandiosity, whichever it was, only sharpened his nervousness.

Douglass had kept his side of the bargain. Sitting and waiting as the three of them arrived was as senior a group as he'd ever lectured: the deputy secretary of defense, the chairman of the Joint Chiefs of Staff, and—listening on an encrypted channel from Tokyo, where he'd been dispatched to reassure the Asian allies of America's security obligations—the four-star admiral in charge of Indo-Pacific Command. Willoughby also noticed two midgrade officers in the back of the room, an Air Force colonel and a Navy captain, probably the Joint Staff officers who had adapted his study for the war plan.

It occurred to Willoughby that there were no Marines in the room and just one civilian official—which worried him. A key role of civilian experts in the Pentagon was to shield a defense secretary from the onslaught of the uniformed military's self-aggrandizing advice. Through the years, a few secretaries who'd come to the job from the corporate world ignored their civilian underlings, seeing them the way that CEOs viewed administrators, and thus turned for advice almost exclusively to the generals, on the premise that, being generals, they possessed the expertise. If Portis was following suit, he was doing so at his peril; he was going to get boxed in to gold-plated weapons, inflated threat estimates, and, in the event of war, bloated troop deployments and rosy-eyed optimism.

This was especially so, given the current stable of generals. The Joint Chiefs chairman, a leftover from the previous administration, was particularly worrisome. Montgomery Vollmer, an Air Force general, was the most brilliant *and* most hawkish chairman that Willoughby had ever met—an unusual combination. The super hawks from Cold War times tended to be dunderheads; the academically credentialed four-star officers of modern times tended to be relatively moderate. Vollmer was both highly educated—master's degree from Georgetown, doctorate from Harvard—and fiercely bellicose. He had been calling for a huge arms buildup in Asia to counter what he forecast as imminent aggression by Beijing—in some forums, he advocated a preemptive attack against China—and he was all too calmly sanguine about the strategic benefits of small-scale nuclear strikes ("escalate to de-escalate" and "punish to deter" were phrases he would casually invoke). He looked the part, as well: trim, muscular, grim faced.

Willoughby had spent much of his hour-long walk to the Capitol earlier that afternoon mulling over the basic contours of this speech, though not the fine details. He couldn't repeat what he had said so bluntly to Douglass and Portis—that, soon after writing the study that was now the basis for the official war plan, he wrote a critique of the same study. He didn't know whether any of the people in the room had been briefed on Willoughby's peculiar business model. In any case, explicitly laying it out, especially as the men in the room (and they were all men) were putting the war plan into motion, would wreck his credibility, paint himself as someone unworthy of trust, and it would permit them—the ones who would soon be making decisions and advising the president—to dismiss whatever portions of his talk they were predisposed to dismiss. Total honesty, in short, would be not just a potential career-buster but counterproductive to the mission at hand. Now, though, seeing Vollmer in the room, Willoughby was unsure whether to confront the general's views directly or ignore them, going over his head to address the secretary and Douglass.

Portis tersely introduced Willoughby, who rose to speak. "Thank you, Mr. Secretary," he began. "I want to thank all of you for coming today, and for the respect that you've shown my study by adopting it as the basis of your current planning, but I should warn you against paying it too much respect. Three years ago, the Air Force and the Navy asked me to write the rationale for a revised military operations plan—the O Plan—for a possible war with China, and that is what I did. As you all know, O Plans generally do not include an assessment of the risks or the likelihood of success, and so neither did my study.

Under the circumstances, I now feel duty bound to outline those risks, some of which occurred to me while doing the study, some in the intervening few years as the military balance between the United States and China has shifted."

Willoughby did not mention the study he'd done for the Marines (Douglass had assured him that no one in the room was likely aware of it), and in that sense, his rationale for being in the room was shady. He noticed Portis scowling and shaking his head slightly, but Portis had already sized him up as an intellectual racketeer, no more or less depraved than the town's other racketeers, so he didn't let the disdainful expression bother him. However, quite aside from his motive, Willoughby's point (or so he now rationalized to himself) was legitimate: he *had* written the outlines of an O Plan; it *was* the best O Plan that he could come up with, maybe the best that *anyone* could come up with, as evidenced by the fact that the Pentagon's top officers were about to adopt it as the real-life war plan. But that didn't mean it was flawless, and he was here to enumerate the flaws and the risks of following its guidelines.

He went on, "One assumption of my study—and, I take it, of the O Plan—is that we will be able to mobilize substantial air and naval forces over a period of two to three weeks before full-scale combat begins. If we are allowed that much time, we would indeed be able to meet and probably defeat a Chinese offensive in the Taiwan Strait or the South China Sea. However, China may not give us that much time. Since writing my study, it has become *increasingly* clear"—actually it was clear *enough* at the time, as Willoughby noted in the study for the Marines, but no point dwelling on this now—"that the forces we *presently* have in the region can be overwhelmed from many angles by myriad Chinese munitions. These include anti-ship cruise missiles, drones, mines, antiaircraft batteries, as well as cyber offensive capabilities that can blind our radar, our guided missiles, and our data links to GPS satellites.

He rattled on: "I should also emphasize, my study outlined a way to achieve 'escalation dominance.' It assumed that, at each phase of combat, on each rung of the escalation ladder, we would remain dominant—we would be ahead, and, given that fact, the Chinese would not want to keep climbing the ladder, only to be met with greater levels of destruction and ultimately with defeat. Again, if they give us two or three weeks to prepare for battle, we would likely attain that edge. However, if they see us mobilizing for full-scale war, they will be tempted to exploit their short-term advantage and escalate to full-scale war before we are in a good position to respond."

He paused and and looked around the room, to gauge how things were going. He couldn't tell. It was like an oil painting out there, everyone motionless, poker-faced. He needed to step things up a notch.

"At the moment," he said, raising his voice a few decibels, "the Chinese seem to be merely *matching* our moves, just as we seem to be *matching* theirs, not yet seeking *dominance*, much less *rapid* dominance. In other words, we both have a chance to back down."

That got some eyes blinking, some heads twisting around, even a cough and an intake of breath or two. Willoughby had crossed a line. He was shifting gears, away from pure military-technical analysis—what's the best way to win the war with the resources at hand—to a broader analysis of *policy*, of the options for war *and peace*.

"If China were attacking the United States or our allies," he kept going, "if it posed an existential threat to our vital interests, then obviously we would have to respond accordingly, even at some risk. But if that isn't what is happening, if the conflict has been triggered by a relatively minor event or some misunderstanding"—here, Willoughby noticed Portis and Douglass glaring at each other—"and if the spiral of escalation can be slowed down or reversed, then I would advise that we take that route before it's too late."

Willoughby had crossed into still deeper untrod territory. Portis had asked him in the limo which of his two studies he believed. Here was his answer. It was the first time in a long time that he'd expressed a belief in *anything*. He felt emboldened to go a step further still.

"I would say one more thing," he ventured. "The ultimate step in a fight for escalation dominance, of course, is nuclear war. In the past, when the United States enjoyed nuclear superiority, that fact deterred many countries from confronting us militarily on *any* level, knowing that we could always pull out the nuclear card. Now, although we vastly outnumber China in nuclear weapons, we don't have superiority in any meaningful sense. In other words, they would still have enough weapons, after a US first strike, to retaliate with catastrophic consequences."

He saw, and for a moment thought he heard, General Vollmer grinding his teeth.

"Now I know," and here Willoughby took a breath, "some in this room believe we still possess nuclear superiority because of our 'left of launch' capabilities."

At this, he detected more glances, coughs, and mumbling. "Left-of-launch" was the term of art for a preemptive strike through cyber means—hacking into the enemy's system so it can't *launch* its missiles rather than attacking the missiles directly. "In effect, it could restore America's days of nuclear superiority, disabling an enemy's ability to retaliate to an attack; it could, in short, enable escalation dominance.

"However," he continued, "I'm sure many of you know there is no cause for high confidence in our left-of-launch capabilities." Willoughby then paraphrased what Gupta had told him on the phone earlier that afternoon, which is what a senior Cyber Command officer had told Gupta at the RAND Corporation: that the US had tested left-of-launch against Chinese missiles; that some attempts seemed to work, but others did not; and it wasn't entirely clear whether those that seemed to work actually did.

"In other words," he said with uncharacteristic stress in his voice, "it would be an extremely high risk to go into an escalation-dominance contest, believing that we had a nuclear trump card to play in the final round. We might not."

No one from Cyber Command was present, but Willoughby noticed that the two mid-grade officers in the back of the room glanced at each other, raised their eyebrows, and exchanged some whispered commentary. He couldn't tell from lip reading or their body language or any other clues whether they were affirming his doubts or dismissing them.

Willoughby figured it was time to wrap things up. "Thank you once again for inviting me to address you," he said. "I would be pleased and honored to take any questions you might have."

The room turned even quieter than before. The flutter of a small motorboat could be heard through the double-paned windows overlooking the Potomac.

"Thank you for coming in, Dr. Willoughby," Portis said, nodding to Douglass, who rose from his chair, walked toward Willoughby, and led him out of the room.

So that was it. No questions. Willoughby felt used. Had Portis and Douglass complied so quickly with his request to brief them on the downside of a war, so they could *say*—to themselves and to their political masters in the White House and Congress—that they'd been briefed on the case against escalation and could, therefore, go to war in good conscience without further debate? It seemed so. Willoughby had spent much of his career gaming clients; maybe it was only fair that he too should get gamed now and then. Still, the stakes were a lot higher this time out; he'd expected, perhaps naively, a more serious hearing.

Douglass was silent during their walk to the building's River Exit. As they approached the doors, he said, "Our driver will take you wherever you'd like to go." He paused for a few seconds. "I'll keep you posted." They shook hands, and his friend turned away to go back to the secretary.

A half hour later, just minutes after Willoughby got back to his office, the phone rang. It was Douglass. "I thought you'd like to know that, much as the secretary and the chairman appreciated your points, they're going to advise the president to proceed with the O Plan as it stands. They wanted me to assure you that they will act with considerable caution, the higher they climb the escalation ladder, especially as they approach the nuclear threshold."

"I hope that would be the case, even if I hadn't given my talk," Willoughby said, a slight shudder in his voice.

"Thanks again, Serge," Douglass replied. "Take care."

It was almost 5:00, and Willoughby was ready for a drink. He'd wasted the whole day, trying to ward off a war that he seemed responsible for starting—trying to "save the planet," as Natalie Gold had implored him to do the night before, something he'd never tried doing for the previous forty years, in part because he regarded the whole notion as a fool's fantasy. And yet he felt disappointed, even distressed, that he'd failed.

He phoned Gold. "They didn't buy my revised briefing," he said. "It looks like they're going to war."

"So I hear," Gold replied.

Willoughby wondered how she'd found out so quickly. "Do you want to go for an early dinner?"

"It's five o'clock," she replied. "Where do you live, *Florida?* How about a normal dinner, say, at eight o'clock?"

They met at the same rooftop restaurant, and sat at the same slightly remote table, where, just two nights earlier, Chas Greenway rushed out in a fit after Willoughby asked him about the Chinese spies phoning the hardware store in Maryland.

Gold was wearing a casual outfit, similar to the one she'd worn to his apartment the night before, but in a warm grey instead of black. They talked for a while in personal, slightly flirtatious tones, as if they were just an ordinary man and woman out for an evening getting to know one another and the world wasn't on the verge of being blown to smithereens.

"So, Serge," Gold began, "tell me some things about you that I don't already know. For starters, how did a Willoughby get a name like Serge?"

He smiled and gave her the short version of the tale about his off-the-grid parents and his childhood at an anarcho-syndicalist commune.

"Was it common for these children to be named after foreign revolutionaries?" she asked, a bit incredulous.

"Oh, yes," Willoughby replied. "I had a close playmate, all through my grade-school years, named Marx Koufax."

"You did not," Gold said.

"Yes, I did," Willoughby insisted gently. "Another friend was named Lenin Henderson."

"What are these poor boys doing now?"

"I lost track of Len. He moved away when his parents accused their fellow travelers of petty bourgeois deviationism. But I've kept in touch with Marx. Last I heard, he was in private equity. Made a fortune from cobalt mines and tech start-ups."

"So, getting into math and defense studies was *your* form of rebellion?" Gold asked.

"Yes, when I was about ten, some of my friends and I discovered books that our parents had stashed away." Willoughby looked down, took another drink, and paused, as if to dredge up a chestful of buried memories. "My dad—and I only learned this later—had been all set to be a mathematician before dropping out. He'd seen ultimate truth in numbers before he found a more class-conscious truth in liberation ideology. Going through some boxes one day, I discovered his old textbooks on number theory, statistics, and calculus, and they gripped me right away. I didn't see much *truth or liberation* in the way my parents and their comrades were living. Math looked like a good escape to solid ground. And I was good at it. I understood all the concepts, solved problems quickly, and devised games testing myself, like memorizing the decimal places of *pi*—I think I worked up to thirty-six. Then when I got to college, exposing myself to the world for the first time, I was taught that math could be used to solve real problems. That was a thrill, for several years. I also found some art and design monographs—it turned out my mother was going to be a fine arts major—and I had never seen anything so beautiful. Beauty for its own sake—a revelation. The first thing I did, once I got off the commune, was go to an art museum."

"Are your parents still around?" Gold asked.

"No," he replied, lowering his voice. "My mother died of breast cancer quite young, in her forties. My father was so distressed, not just by her death but its randomness. His worldview was so locked into systems that supposedly explained everything, he'd lost all awareness of chance or mystery—and here was the ultimate chance and mystery. Over the next several years, he drank himself to death."

Willoughby had never talked about this with anyone, not in such detail. Now that he'd brought it up, he realized why Gold's challenge from the other night—"What's your *purpose* in life?"—had hit such a nerve. He now recalled, but didn't dare mention (the memory was still awkward and painful) his final conversation with his father. The commune had long ago broken up, but his dad stayed as far off the grid as he could. He settled in a ramshackle cabin, not quite in the middle of nowhere, but you could see it from there. Rousing himself from a stupor on the last night of Serge's last weekend visit, he gazed at his son and mumbled, "I have no purpose." He had glommed onto revolutionary ideology because it combined the certainty that he valued in mathematics with a social-political-existential purpose, something that numbers, though eloquently precise, lacked; and now his wife's—Serge's mother's—meaningless death revealed his core beliefs as illusions.

Long before that final visit, Serge had rejected a life on the edge and reconciled himself to a cosmic backdrop of purposelessness against which he felt free to pursue his own aims and pleasures. But now, speaking of this history out loud, against the setting of an impending catastrophe brought on by his own insouciance, he wondered whether the rejection of his parents' dreams really required, as he'd thought it did, an utter abandonment of purpose and any sense of social, political, or moral… what was the word he was seeking… *responsibility.*

There was a long pause. "What about you?" Willoughby asked, breaking the silence. "What's your origin story?"

"I grew up in Manhattan, on the Upper West Side," Gold began. "My mother worked at the New York Public Library. She was one of the women who researched the answers to any and all questions that people phoned in to ask. As I kid, I found this magical—the idea that all the facts were out there and that, if you looked through enough books or magazines or whatever, you'd find them.

"My father was a professor of physics at Columbia—not the 'flaky, out to lunch, loop-de-loops of six-dimensional string theory,' as he put it. I mean, he found the idea interesting, he was colleagues with some of its originators, he had lengthy, civil conversations with them. But the whole theory was impossible to verify and therefore, by definition, it was not science. He once told me, 'Maybe I won't discover the Grand Unified Theory of the universe, but the stuff I study is wondrous enough'—the elements of real, solid, *applied* physics: thermodynamics, electromagnetism, optics, acoustics, high-energy particles."

She spoke so fluently, as if delivering a biographical lecture. Willoughby figured she must have recited it many times before. But then she paused, looked down, hesitated with her mouth half open.

"And yes," she went on," "he worked on nuclear weapons too, but for only a few years, quitting that business after fully realizing its dead-end consequences."

She took a few more sips of her wine, then swallowed the rest of it. Willoughby was impressed. In one sense, his life story and Gold's could not be more different. Her career was an extension of her parents' influences, while his was an abject repudiation. Yet it was startling that, coming from such different places, they both wound up in the enterprise of chasing concrete facts. The difference was that Natalie and her father found pleasure *and* purpose in their indifference toward outsized theory and their pursuit of verifiable facts, while Serge's father was left with no brand of meaning or satisfaction once his grand theory went up in smoke, and Serge himself was only beginning to grapple with the value of *purpose* and whether it was possible to pursue both purpose and pleasure. Perhaps, Willoughby mused, really for the first time, his life *hadn't* been such a rebellion against his parents after all; maybe he was cut from the same cloth as his father and suffered more than he'd ever considered from the same evasions and false certainties.

They both sat silent. A pall seemed to hang over the air, as if they both felt uncomfortable exposing so much premature intimacy.

"Anyway," said Gold, after taking a hefty swig from her refilled wine glass, "I worked for a couple of newspapers, but couldn't stand the hierarchies, didn't want to be told what sorts of stories I could and couldn't write. One time, I landed a big scoop on a military scandal. My editors assigned the follow-up story to one of the regular reporters on the Pentagon beat—a man, naturally—and I quit. Blogs were becoming a thing, so I started one and figured out how to monetize it with advertising. I came to dislike the dependency of that business model, but stuck with it long enough to cultivate a black book full of sources. Then I switched to a subscription model, raised the price, limited the readership, and added passcodes to polish the patina of exclusivity. That swelled my reputation among the cognoscenti, who supplied me with still more scoops, and, well, my business took off."

After another pause, Gold shifted in her seat, straightening up and leaning back. "Now let's talk war and peace," she said, confirming Willoughby's detection of a shift in the conversation from personal to professional. "From what I've learned in the past couple hours, there's more going on here than we've assumed. I haven't got to the bottom of it, but there's a bureaucratic battle going on inside the military and the intelligence agencies. One faction wants to confront China's ambitions head on, even if it means risking a major war. You met with some leaders of that faction today. Another faction wants to engage more diplomatically with China, and within that faction there are at least two groups. The first subgroup wants to draft arms control treaties, nonaggression pacts, that sort of thing. The second wants to negotiate a grand bargain, a nineteenth-century concept of peace, where the ruling elites in Beijing and Washington meet at some palace in Vienna and divvy up the globe into two spheres of influence."

"Would that work?" Willoughby asked.

"I don't know, *you've* got the Ph.D. in political science," Gold shot back, only half laughing. "One thing I do know: that some senior intelligence officials form the main anti-war faction, and they're having a hard time resisting the Pentagon, in part because, as you know, it's hard to resist the Pentagon, in part because the CIA itself is split into those two groups—the conventional arms controllers versus the ambitious empire builders—so they haven't been able to mount a united front, much less corral other agencies to join their team."

Gold paused to drain her glass of white Burgundy, looked Willoughby straight on, and said, "I think you should go meet with the director of the CIA."

"Danica Bloom?" Willoughby asked, a little startled.

"Yes," Gold said. "You know her, right?"

Willoughby wondered how long Gold had been waiting to throw that name on the table. Yes, he knew Danica Bloom, all right. She and Willoughby had been an item long ago. They met (where else?) at a Washington party midway into Willoughby's career as a consultant, when Bloom—a decade younger and closer to the start of her shimmy up the pole of power—was a senior staffer on the Senate Foreign Relations Committee. They dated for several months. The sex was spectacular, but, aside from that, they didn't like doing any of the same things. She hated sports, except for tournament croquet, which he found bafflingly dull. He fell asleep at the opera; she groaned and fidgeted all through *A Night at the Opera*. She detested almost all art after the mid-nineteenth century; he didn't see the point of much art before then. They drifted apart and hadn't spoken in all the years since, seeing each other only a few times in passing from a distance. He'd sent her messages of congratulations upon each of her subsequent promotions—assistant secretary of state, senior director of the National Security Council staff, ambassador to NATO, and finally top spymaster at Langley. But she'd never replied.

"I'm pretty sure Danica Bloom wouldn't see me," Willoughby said.

"I'm pretty sure she would, under the circumstances," Gold replied.

"What are the circumstances?"

"The circumstances," Gold replied, flashing a self-satisfied grin, "are that Danica is the leader of the anti-war faction, and her chief emissary to the Chinese is Wolf Mandelbaum."

CHAPTER 5

Willoughby set out at 7:00 the next morning to make an 8:00 breakfast with Danica Bloom at a small Chinese café called Xin Hua-Yuan, located in the outer Virginia suburbs at the cul-de-sac of a dusty serpentine back road so narrow that he marveled it showed up on Google Maps.

Gold had briefed him on the place ahead of time. Officially it appeared to be owned by a local businessman, the descendent of Taiwanese immigrants, who also operated a nearby dry cleaner. But the real owner was the nephew of a Beijing apparatchik who, three decades earlier, had created a Chinese-American consortium that set up a restaurant called Sichuan Garden, one of the most elegant, acclaimed, and infamous eateries in the history of Washington DC. Its kitchen had boasted two of mainland China's top ten chefs, who served, by wide consensus, the best Asian cuisine on the East Coast. Willoughby remembered the place well. It was located just south of DuPont Circle. This was before he moved to that neighborhood, but Giles Molloy took him there for lunch a few times, and he could still summon its savory scents and flavors. In the mid-'80s, just a few years into its wildly successful run, Michael Kinsley, the town's smartest political columnist, wrote an exposé revealing that the restaurant's employees were treated like slaves, locked up in a dingy tenement and forbidden from going out on their own or learning English. The article provoked such outrage that the consortium's American partners pulled out, the chefs were ferried back to China, and, after a few weeks of churning out mediocre food at the same outlandish prices, the place shut down. Many in the D.C. establishment, including liberals who otherwise fancied themselves human rights advocates, were deeply pissed at Kinsley. Willoughby recalled a mutual friend fuming, "Mike makes *one* foray into investigative journalism, and he decides to destroy not some craven bureaucrat or corrupt politician but this town's only great restaurant?"

Now the co-owner's nephew was running his own joint venture—Xin Hua-Yuan was Mandarin for "New Garden"—though, alas, without the imported chefs. (According to Gold, the food was so-so.) The place operated mainly as a hangout for a hodgepodge of spies, brokers, and venture capitalists looking to trade gossip and make deals away from the purview of the town's standard gatekeepers. The concept made no sense to Willoughby: wouldn't the gatekeepers start hanging out there, if just to see who was making the back-channel deals, especially in these times of tensions with Beijing? According to Gold, the Chinese didn't care who was watching. (This rang true: during one of Willoughby's few projects on cyber warfare, he discovered that, unlike the Russians, who devised slyly surreptitious methods of subverting Western computer networks, the Chinese hacked in the open.) Meanwhile, as word of the café's true function spread to its intended clientele, Xin Hua-Yuan did much more business than it otherwise would have.

Willoughby arrived on the dot of 8:00, which he'd been told was before the normal breakfast pack showed up—in fact, no other customers were there—but even so, he was ushered to the back of the place, up a flight of rickety stairs, across a dimly lit corridor, and into a small, stark room adorned only by a Chinese calendar on the wall and a small plastic statue of Buddha on a shelf.

Danica Bloom was sitting at the room's only table. Standing nearby were three security agents, one of whom searched Willoughby, presumably for weapons and wires.

"Hi, Danica, nice digs you've got here," Willoughby said, trying to come off casually witty, as he'd done during the old days, but he realized the tone was off key. She stood, and the two approached each other awkwardly, at first moving hesitantly toward a hug, but winding up with a handshake and a light pat on each other's shoulders before sitting down.

"Sorry, Serge," she said, smiling just enough to avoid being rude, "I would have met you in my office at Langley, but, as I'll explain to you, the internecine warfare is raging, and someone's keeping close tabs on the visitors' logs."

She hadn't changed much, except for her hair, which was shorter and greyer. Otherwise, she was still short, trim, and intense, her voice insistent, her eyes focused, as if taking in everything and scouting all the angles.

Without looking at a menu (there was none on the table), she ordered for both of them—Willoughby couldn't decipher just what kind of food—then started talking at a rapid clip.

"So," she said, "you know that Wolf Mandelbaum has been arrested and detained on *suspicion* of espionage—not *charged*, he hasn't been formally *charged* with anything. There's no way he could be a Chinese spy. In fact, he's the exact opposite."

Willoughby tilted his head in a mix of curiosity and confusion.

Bloom paused and slowed down. "A little background. You may recall news stories a few months ago about growing tensions between the US and China—their planes buzzing our aircraft carriers, our submarines crossing into their waters. Things were more dangerous than anyone reported. We really almost went to war. Then the clashes stopped. That's because, for several weeks now, some of us in government have been running back-channel communications with China, trying to reduce tensions. I am the prime mover, the top American official, on this back channel. Wolf has been the main go-between. I think Natalie Gold has told you that much—I *authorized* her to tell you that much. Here is what she has not told you."

Bloom paused while the waiter brought in platters of food, mainly various dumplings and sauces. Meanwhile, Willoughby was stunned by the Natalie Gold connection. How long had they been talking to each other, he wondered.

After the waiter went back to the kitchen, Bloom resumed talking.

"The officials who oppose the existence of this back channel—mainly in the Pentagon, but also a few in the FBI, the State Department, and a couple branches of the intelligence community—have been trying to cough up dirt on Wolf, any evidence that paints him as a traitor or a turncoat. They couldn't find anything, until this crazy phone call from his house to the hardware store in Maryland."

Willoughby braced himself for the lecturing, the yelling, the threats of a possible jail sentence.

"Natalie says you were a guest at a party at Wolf's house the night of the phone call," she went on, more calmly than he'd expected.

"Wolf did not make that call—I'm convinced of that. I need you to help me find out who did."

Willoughby sat there, puzzled. Was it possible Gold did not tell her that *he* had made the phone call? Or had she told her, but now Bloom was toying with him, maneuvering him into a trap—but what sort of trap?

"I don't understand, Danica," he finally said, choosing to go along with the pretense (if that's what it was) that she didn't know he was the culprit. "You're the director of the CIA. Why can't *you* find out who made the call?"

"Because, believe it or not, Serge, I have no legal authority to spy on American citizens," she said dryly. "Ordinarily, I would formally request assistance from the FBI and get it done that way, but they're not cooperating. Because Wolf is now seen as a spy, they think that I'm naïve at best and very possibly a spy or a Chinese stooge myself."

"This sounds crazy," Willoughby said, not knowing what else to say.

"It *is* crazy," Bloom said. "There's a very secretive counterintelligence unit within the FBI that's up to its ears in the operation against the Chinese hardware store *and* against Wolf Mandelbaum, and they're squeezing me out of the highest-level intelligence related to China."

Bloom had misunderstood his remark. It wasn't that Willoughby thought the FBI's resistance was crazy; he thought the *whole story* was crazy.

"Wait, wait, let's step back a bit," he said. "How did Wolf Mandelbaum become the go-between in a back channel with China?"

"It's complicated," Bloom said. "I'm telling you this because I need you to trust me, so I can trust you to do the right thing. Wolf's wife, Chae-won, has a cousin who's high up in South Korean intelligence. He's in the movement that's very keen to open up relations with North Korea. For years, he's been cultivating good relations with Beijing to promote that goal. When our own tensions with China started ratcheting up, this cousin reached out to his top Beijing contact and offered mediation with Washington. Beijing was interested, but it turned out the cousin was bluffing. He didn't have any connections here, so he contacted Chae-won, who told Wolf, who came to me. One of Wolf's most recent consulting contracts was with CIA, and while no one was terribly impressed with his work, we knew that he had fans in the Chinese ministry of national defense. Some of its senior officers, who'd risen through the ranks during their own cold war with Moscow, venerated Wolf for his papers on the Russian military threat. The cousin put Wolf in touch with his Beijing contacts, through Chae-won. Wolf came to me—and, by the way, he told the Chinese he was bringing me into the discussions, which wouldn't have had any impact if they'd stayed purely private."

Bloom ate a dumpling and drank some tea. Willoughby, was impressed how calmly she laid out the Byzantine maze of her daily routines.

"We were making progress," she went on. "Then came the phone call. Some officials in the Pentagon, the NSA, and the FBI—all skeptics of the back channel from the beginning—saw this as proof that Wolf was a Chinese spy all along, or at least a tool. Meanwhile, the cousin's contacts in Beijing took Wolf's arrest as evidence that the *back channel* wasn't real, that it was either run by a faction that didn't represent US policy or, more likely, a conniving ploy to coax China into letting down its guard while the American jackals prepared to attack.

"That's why we're on the brink of war," Bloom concluded. "The Chinese think Wolf's arrest means the peace channel was an *American* trick. Some Americans think the phone call from Wolf's house means the peace channel was a *Chinese* trick. As a result, each side thinks it has to mobilize for war before the other side mobilizes for war. I have to show both sides that Wolf did not make that phone call, that the peace channel was real, that the arrest was a mistake, and so the war can be called off. I need you to help me out."

Only now did Willoughby fully realize the tragicomic scope of the shitstorm that he'd unleashed with his phone prank at Mandelbaum's. "What can I do?" he asked in as responsible a tone as he could muster.

"Make a list of who was at that party," she replied. "If there were people you saw but don't know, ask people you *do* know if *they* know them. Then please give me the list. I know you're under no obligation to cooperate with us on this. I know that people in your field are supposed to steer clear of this sort of thing. But this is about war and peace—it's about trying to avert catastrophe. I know you don't believe in much, but I'm hoping you believe in that."

"I'm working on it," he said.

"That's what I hear."

Willoughby walked to his car in a daze. What was *that* about? Was it *all* real? Her closing line—"That's what I hear"—she must have heard it from Gold. What else did she hear? Did she really not know that he made the call from Mandelbaum's phone? He thought about running back into the restaurant and fessing up, but he wasn't ready just yet to commit professional suicide (if Gold hadn't told Bloom, Bloom would certainly tell others) or possibly face criminal charges (*was* his prank illegal? ...he should probably look into that). Maybe it wouldn't make a difference anyway. Now that his briefing at the Pentagon had placed him firmly on the side of the anti-war faction (which at the time he didn't know existed), would Portis and the generals even believe his confession? Would they think he was putting his body on the line for the cause, which would be pretty funny, as Willoughby had never done that for any cause in his entire life.

Meanwhile, the breakfast with Bloom had intensified Willoughby's self-loathing: not only had his phone call from Mandelbaum's (a moronic, juvenile prank, quite apart from its consequences) sparked a possible war between the world's two most powerful rivals; it was also discrediting the one woman (an upstanding, brilliant woman, quite apart from his own checkered history with her) who might otherwise be in a position to stop the conflict from spiraling out of control.

At the same time, this cascading sensation of embarrassment, loyalty, patriotism, and responsibility—here was that word popping up in his mind again, *responsibility*, sending a shock of the new through his nervous system, a fearsome, ennobling sensation that he hadn't felt in decades—compelled Willoughby to do *something* to clear up this grand mess of his own making.

He wasn't going to draw up a list of party guests, as Bloom had suggested; that would be pointless. He did know one way to exonerate Mandelbaum—and restore Bloom's power—without incriminating himself. But to do that, he needed to get in touch with Chas Greenway, his friend (now ex-friend?), whose drunken indiscretion set this tale in motion.

As soon as he got back to his office, after his hour-long drive from his breakfast with Bloom, his new assistant, Vijay Gupta, knocked on his door. The previous night, he had instructed Gupta to monitor all newscasts and official statements for twists and turns in the conflict with China. Gupta was ready to recite a boiled down summary of several hours' worth of monitoring the media and taking notes.

"Manny Slaughter!" Willoughby shouted to his more senior assistant in the next office. "You might want to come here and listen to this."

Slaughter was emerging as the office's IT specialist. As a test during his job interview, he was asked to find out as much as he could about Willoughby, himself, in five minutes' time. He found everything: Willoughby's date and place of birth, every address where he'd ever lived as a bills-paying adult, which magazines he subscribed to, even his Social Security number. Ever since his hire, Slaughter had dug up valuable material on dozens of projects with similarly mind-numbing speed and depth. By contrast, Gupta was shaping up to be the shop's policy aide, and Slaughter had no problem with that division of responsibility.

Gupta shifted a bit in discomfort, not expecting an audience, especially one that included Slaughter, who, though only a few years older, intimidated the new assistant. "Do you want me to display some visual aids as I talk?" Gupta asked, holding up a thumb drive. "I have recorded a few news clips."

"No," Willoughby replied, barely holding in a laugh. "Very enterprising, but not necessary. Just give us the headlines."

"OK then," Gupta said and read down the list.

The US Navy was moving another aircraft carrier into the South China Sea.

Chinese merchant marine ships, docked across the strait from Taiwan, were now almost fully loaded with combat troops.

A Taiwanese reconnaissance plane came under fire while flying over the coastline.

Sources confirmed the previous day's suspicions that a malfunctioning American spy satellite had in fact been disabled by a Chinese anti-satellite rocket.

Meanwhile, electric power grids flickered off and on in a few medium-sized cities in both the United States and China—disruptions widely seen as shot-across-the-bow warnings, by both sides, of larger cyberattacks to come.

North Korea, possibly under China's orders, certainly with its complicity, began troop exercises thirty miles north of the South Korean border and test-fired three medium-range ballistic missiles toward Japan, two falling into the East China Sea, the other flying over Japanese territory before crashing into the Pacific Ocean—moves that would no doubt compel the United States to keep substantial military forces bottled up in northeast Asia, for the protection of Japan and South Korea, rather than diverting them southward toward Taiwan.

It was also reported, though not yet confirmed, that China asked Iran to make aggressive moves on oil tankers in the Strait of Hormuz, in an attempt to keep some US warships bottled up in the Middle East. The news source reported that Tehran had not yet responded to Beijing's request.

An impressive summary, Willoughby thought. More to the point, it suggested that things were progressing pretty much as his three-year-old paper had outlined. The good news was that each side was still roughly *matching* the other side's moves; neither side had yet upped the stakes in a move toward escalation *dominance*. Maybe his briefing at the Pentagon had made an impact. In any case, the

Chinese didn't seem to be going for the quick knockout punch that would be their best hope for victory against the United States armed forces. Willoughby took this as a possible sign that they didn't want a war—that they'd welcome an overture to wind the conflict down.

In other words, Willoughby still had some time, but probably not much time. At some point soon, before the Americans had fully mobilized, the Chinese would face a decision—either to go for the quick knockout punch or risk suffering enormous damage and likely defeat if they waited any longer. For a peace overture to be effective, it would have to be offered before that pivot point was reached.

Willoughby phoned Gold to check in and tell her how the meeting went with Bloom, though he suspected she already knew. No one answered. He texted her. No reply. Clearly she was busy. He figured defense reporters don't get a looming war this large very often; when they did, they had no time for anything else. He'd try again later. Still, he wondered if Gold was avoiding him, now that he knew about her Bloom connection.

At 6:00, Willoughby called Chas Greenway. No one answered. He tried again. This time, someone picked up the phone, then hung up right away. He understood why Chas wouldn't want to talk with him. But they needed to talk, so Willoughby drove to his house.

Greenway lived in a leafy Maryland suburb, a few miles north of the D.C. line, on a tidy street completely bereft of human activity. It was as if a neutron bomb had gone off, or he'd stumbled onto a favored tract of the witness protection program. Willoughby wondered how people *lived* like this.

He rang the doorbell. Greenway answered. "I'm not wired," Willoughby said, holding his suit jacket wide open.

Greenway sighed and let him in. The place was a mess: crumb-splattered dishes and smudge-stained glasses on the coffee table, newspapers flung on the floor, a huge dust ball in a corner, the stench of rotten fruit or possibly a dead mouse decaying behind some floorboard in the kitchen.

"Where's Carolyn?" Willoughby asked.

"She's visiting her mother," Greenway replied listlessly. Willoughby suspected this wasn't the whole truth. The marital situation did not seem harmonious.

"We need to talk," he began.

"Did I really tell you about the Chinese agents and the phone calls to the hardware store?" Greenway asked in a desperate tone.

"Yes, you also told me the hardware store's phone number," Willoughby replied calmly.

"Oh, shit!" Greenway moaned. "Honestly, Serge, I don't remember saying those things. I must have blacked out. Jesus, I'm a serious security risk. I need to quit my job."

"I agree. But before you quit, we need to clear up the situation with Wolf Mandelbaum."

Greenway, who'd been pacing the room, stopped short. "Did I tell you about Mandelbaum too?"

"No, I've learned about that part of the story since. That's what we need to talk about."

He sat Greenway down and told him about the night of the party, his prank phone call, Mandelbaum's arrest the next day, and the war clouds that followed.

"You're the only person I've told this to," Willoughby said, which was *technically* true, as Gold, who also knew the story, had figured it out on her own. "I'm telling you, so that now we both have nasty goods on each other. This means we can work together in trust, because if we don't cooperate, if one of us betrays the other, the other can bite back."

"Ah, mutually assured destruction," Greenway said. "So you remember Nuclear Deterrence 101."

"I guess that's our situation, but I hope without the Cold War hostility. The thing is this: we need to prove, with physical evidence, that Wolf was not the guy who made that phone call."

"That will be tough," Greenway said. "You know, when the NSA intercepts phone calls, we just look at the phone numbers involved. If someone else had borrowed or stolen the phone, we wouldn't necessarily know that. Finding out whether that happened requires another level of digging."

"But aren't you in a position to do that digging?"

"Yeah, theoretically."

"We know that, as a player in the CIA's back channel, Mandelbaum talked on the phone several times with officials in China's embassy here and in its UN mission. Since NSA routinely intercepts all communications with foreign officials, you would have records of those calls, right? I mean you personally would have access to those records—not just the transcripts, but the tapes?"

"Yeah, I'm high up in running the whole operation."

"So, we know Mandelbaum didn't make the call that night from his phone. Can you examine the tape of that call, compare it with the tapes of Mandelbaum's calls with Chinese officials from the same phone, and show that the two voices are not the same?"

"That's possible," Greenway said. "Thing is, anytime I do anything with intercepts where US citizens are on the call, an auditor is watching everything I do, and a lawyer is writing down everything the auditor sees. I'd have to come up with a damn good reason to go back to the tapes, or I'd have to do it on the sly. Either way, it's risky."

"What have you got to lose?" Willoughby said with a wry grin and a shrug. He thanked his old friend, shook his hand, clenched his shoulder, and turned to leave.

"One thing, Serge," Greenway said. "Let's say that it *was* you on the phone that night. We might identify that voice as yours."

Willoughby thought for a moment. "Actually, I doubt that you could," he said. "I don't have any foreign clients. I rarely talk on the phone with people in other countries. So, if it's true that you guys save only the intercepts of phone calls with foreigners, I don't think I'm in your files."

"But if you are?"

Willoughby reflected for a moment. "Then we're both in trouble."

Driving back to the city, Willoughby shifted uneasily in his seat, wondering if he'd been too nonchalant with his old friend, if he should have stayed longer, sat down, nursed a brandy with him, asked about his clearly troubled marriage, and discussed more deeply their shared distress over the catastrophe—personal and global—that their mischievous indiscretions might unleash.

Their friendship, long as it was, had never sported a therapeutic dimension. Neither of them was particularly introspective; emotional issues tended to be briefly laughed away or brushed aside. Greenway was older by a couple of years, but they were both younger than most of their grad school classmates, and they were both math prodigies, Willoughby immersed in pure mathematics, Greenway more in computer modeling. They regularly attended the monthly late-afternoon seminars, where outside speakers—military officers, civilian officials, think tank analysts, occasionally a congressman—came to talk about arms control or defense issues. Some of the students treated the conclaves as contests to see who among them could cut the speakers down to size most decisively: exposing holes in their logic, fallacies in their premises, non sequiturs in their theses. Willoughby and Greenway were the renowned champs at this savage game.

The professor who sponsored the seminars, Dr. Basil Q. Jackson, encouraged the sport. Willoughby once overheard a bedraggled speaker complaining to Jackson afterward, "That's a cold-blooded pack you've got as students." Willoughby took it as a badge of pride. So did Jackson, who beamed and laughed at the comment.

They were trained to be cold-blooded. Willoughby remembered, early on in grad school, the first time that he worked on "exchange calculations," the antiseptic term for nuclear war simulations—Blue (our side) fires his nukes, Red (the enemy side) fires his nukes: it's an *exchange* of high-intensity nuclear firepower. As Willoughby toted up the numbers, he realized that his first strike killed twenty million Russian citizens, and this was without aiming any weapons at civilian targets; the deaths were "collateral damage," caused by the radioactive fallout from an attack on strictly military targets. The experience, abstract as it was, plunged him into culture shock. He was able to calm himself to sleep only by reading Sherlock Holmes stories, one each night, before getting into bed.

Then, at some point, Dr. Jackson—who later got him the job in Congress (and, he suspected, got Greenway his job at the NSA as well)—gave him some advice. "It's a lot easier if you just eliminate a few zeroes," the professor, who asked his closest students to call him "Dr. Q.," had said with a chuckle. "If you're calculating fatalities, write 'twenty' instead of 'twenty million.'" He scrawled "20,000,000" on the blackboard, then erased the last six zeroes with a blast of laughter. "And for something like the size of the defense budget," he went on, "write 'one hundred' instead of 'one hundred billion,'" scribbling "$100,000,000,000" on the board, then erasing the last nine zeroes. "More manageable, right?" Dr. Q asked his disturbed student. "Make you feel better?"

They both laughed, Willoughby out of genuine and grateful relief.

Soon, even before the time it took to finish the volume of Holmes stories, Willoughby didn't need Conan Doyle as a filter; he'd absorbed the fine art of compartmentalization.

He and Greenway and who knows how many more like them—they were groomed to separate the analysis from the consequences. It was a seamless step from accomplishing that feat to ignoring the consequences altogether. At the time, Willoughby had seen it as a sensible approach to staying sane—and, until recently, still did, to the extent he thought about it at all. Now, though, he wondered if it lay at the root of all the carelessness in the world.

The next morning, Willoughby got an email that appeared to be from Greenway's wife. He was puzzled for a moment, but then remembered the protocol that he and Chas had worked out a couple years earlier, when they were exchanging tips and insights on a project about information warfare. The drill was that Chas would email him from an AOL account that he had long ago set up in his wife's name—an account that he otherwise almost never used and that she never knew existed. He opened the message. It read:

> Looked into that matter. Your friend didn't make any
> of those other calls, either. They came from his phone,
> but the voice was female (his wife?).

The message was vague enough to avoid setting off a keyword alert at Fort Meade, but Willoughby got its gist: Wolf's wife, Chae-won, had made the calls to the Chinese officials; *she* was the back channel, either as a mediator for Wolf or—possibly—going freelance. If the latter, how far had she crawled out on her own branch? Was she working on behalf of the CIA, or did she have her own agenda? A couple of Wolf's friends had mused over the years that Chae-won was the real brains in the Mandelbaum household, but Willoughby had never taken the remark seriously. Now he wondered.

He had no way of contacting Bloom directly, not without triggering alarms among those who, so she claimed, were monitoring her every move. But Gold seemed to have an in. So, he sent Gold a text:

> I need to talk with your friend who I met at the
> Garden.

Ten minutes later, he received a reply:

> OK. Meanwhile, I'm looking for a book of Andy
> Warhol's Polaroids. Could you go to Second Story
> and see if they have a copy. Thanks, NG.

Second Story was the used bookstore where Gold had supposedly bought the volumes of Harold Feinstein's photography and Auden's poetry, but Willoughby figured she was sending him there to pick up something other than a book.

He told Donna Cappella that he needed to go out for some air and strolled over to the shop, avoiding the slightest twitch of urgency; he'd get there fast enough, as it was only two blocks away. Once he arrived, he picked through the New Arrivals shelf near the front desk, as if he had all the time in the world, then ambled to the back of the store, where the art books were arrayed on a long aisle of floor-to-ceiling shelves in alphabetical order. He moved to the section on artists whose last names began with W.

Just then, a slightly disheveled young man with dark hair and thick glasses approached him, looking down at his phone. He bumped into Willoughby, dropped his phone on the floor, leaned down to get it, and, as he was rising back up, slipped the phone into Willoughby's jacket pocket. "Sorry about that," the man said, adding in a whisper, "DB will call soon," presumably referring to Danica Bloom.

Willoughby stayed in the store for another couple minutes, then left. He texted Gold on his own phone:

> No Warhol Polaroids, but picked up something else
> that looks interesting. SW.

He had never played spy games before and was finding it disorientingly fun.

The phone in his pocket, the one that the man had slipped to him in the bookstore, buzzed a few minutes after he got back to the office. It was Bloom. "What's going on? You can speak freely."

He told her that Chae-won, not Wolf, had been talking with the Chinese in the back channel.

"How do you know that?"

Willoughby hesitated, not wanting to give up Greenway just yet, figuring it would be better to wait until after Bloom regained some of her power so she could bring his friend in from the cold, maybe offer him a job at Langley in exchange for his cooperation. "I can't tell you."

"Christ, Serge, for all that I've told *you*?" she snapped.

Willoughby stayed cool, figuring that she hadn't let him in on everything either, especially on what she knew about his own role in this saga. "Let's just say I know someone with access to intercepts.

Timing is crucial to this person too. You'll know everything soon enough."

Bloom sighed, not at all pleased.

He went on, "I thought this person would be able to compare the tape of Wolf's calls to the Chinese at the UN with the call that night to the hardware store, to prove the voices weren't the same, but it turns out Wolf wasn't calling the Chinese, a woman was, presumably Chae-won. So, I have two questions. First, is Chae-won onboard with your operation, or could she be playing her own game?"

"I don't think she's playing a separate game," Bloom said. "I had full access to the transcripts of those calls before I got squeezed out, but names aren't mentioned. The calls came from Wolf's landline, so I figured it was him. I wouldn't have thought it was Chae-won. Regardless, whoever it was, the caller was sticking to the script—a lot of talk about 'verifiable reduction of tensions,' 'confidence-building measures,' the usual diplomatic phrases, nothing untoward, nothing suspicious."

"My second question," Willoughby said, "is this: do *you* have any tapes of Wolf talking? Maybe one of your people listened in on some of his calls and recorded them from your end?"

"No, we *really* can't do that. But let me think." She paused for two seconds. "Last year, he gave a talk here, something about the US-Russia-China power triangle. That definitely would have been recorded. If you could get me a thumb drive of the call to the hardware store, our guys here could compare it with the voice on Wolf's lecture."

"I don't know," Willoughby said, hedging. "That would be asking my source to commit a felony." (More precisely, *another* felony, he thought.) "Could you give me a clip from Wolf's talk at Langley, maybe an unclassified clip, and my source could do the comparison?"

Bloom paused. "None of it was classified, really. I'll text the file to the phone you're using now. When you get it, download it to a thumb drive, then burn the phone. If you need to talk again, do what you did this time. If I need to talk with you, I'll do the same. Thanks, Serge."

She hung up.

Willoughby did as he was told. Later that night, he drove back out to suburbia, handed Greenway the thumb drive, and asked if he could compare Mandelbaum's voice in the speech at Langley with the voice on the phone call to the hardware store. Greenway warned him that the task was complicated. The acoustical differences between a P.A. speaker in a large auditorium and a telephone in a small home office might make it hard to hone in on any differences between the voices, especially with the equipment that Greenway had on his desktop. (He couldn't risk sneaking around with the high-tech gear again.) But he'd give it a try.

The next morning Willoughby got an email from the AOL account of Greenway's wife:

> Sorry, as I suspected might be the case, the acoustical differences overwhelm any differences between the voices. Plus, just to my ears, the two voices sound similar. Were you trying to imitate him on that call?

Dammit, Willoughby now recalled, he *did* imitate Mandelbaum's faux-continental baritone when he phoned the hardware store, for reasons that he couldn't quite fathom at the moment. So here was yet another way that his childish prank was not only setting the world on fire, but also tossing up barriers to those who were trying to douse the flames.

He was beginning to think that he'd come to the end of the line. It looked as if the only way to stop the war was for him to come forward and confess that he'd made the phone call from Mandelbaum's house that night. Otherwise, if Bloom was right, the generals on both sides would continue to believe—for ironically contradictory reasons—that the back-channel peace overture was phony. Willoughby had hoped that Greenway could get him out of the mess the two of them made, but that wasn't going to happen. Coming forward would mean the end of his career, at the very least.

Well, he'd had a good run, racked up some savings, made some good investments. He could sell the condo and move to New York, which, in some ways, he liked better than Washington anyway and where nobody knew the details—only a few knew even the broad outlines—of his professional life.

But he was kidding himself. Ostracism from the society of consultants might not be the worst of the consequences. He could face jail time, and that gave him a shivering pause. Willoughby valued freedom and independence above all else; he'd built his entire life on that principle, forgoing personal and political trappings. Prison, even if just for a year or so in one of those white-collar lockups, would be suffocating.

He looked around his office, which he hadn't had much time to do since this crisis began. To one side were three tall windows letting in streams of light and shadow and air; he couldn't imagine making it through a day for long without windows. The wall across from the windows displayed a row of photographs of jazz musicians. There was John Coltrane, tenor saxophone dangled at an angle, reed in his mouth, the very vision of insouciant intensity; Ella Fitzgerald, belting a song at a nightclub, Duke Ellington in the front row beaming with delight; Thelonious Monk, mouth wide open, fingers pounding a chord new to the universe—all these genius artists radiating a glow of mystery that could mesmerize Willoughby for hours. On the ceiling, a restored antique fan, its oak blades half as wide as the room, scooped the air slowly, more for atmosphere than for cooling.

The rest of Janus Corporation's headquarters looked like most other defense consultancies' offices: the waiting room with a rack of the day's newspapers, a few aerospace journals, the latest issue of *Foreign Affairs*; the corridor walls plastered with old war posters ("Loose Lips Sink Ships," "Keep Calm and Carry On," "Daddy, What Did You Do in the Great War"); his staff's offices were decorated hardly at all.

But Willoughby's space, the last cubbyhole down the hall—off limits to clients, lest they doubt he possessed the single-minded seriousness needed to handle the glumly ominous jobs they were bringing him—was his retreat, a hideaway as much as a workplace, a reflection of his interior life, its sights and sounds a distraction from his workaday drudgery, accessible at a glance whenever he needed them. Turning himself in to the law would mean losing all this too.

He stopped himself short. It was quite the dilemma he was pondering: the fate of the planet versus the comforts of Serge Willoughby. He was embarrassed that he *considered* it a dilemma, and the more he took in that thought, the more it pleased him that he *was* embarrassed. Maybe he was evolving into a good member of civilized society after all. He should probably call his lawyer to see about his options, but first he needed to spill everything to Bloom and figure out, the two of them, how to convince Portis and the generals—and then their Chinese counterparts—that his confession was genuine, that Mandelbaum was neither a turncoat nor a tool, that the back channel was a real thing.

Just then, the phone rang. Willoughby picked it up.

"Doctor Willoughby?" the caller said in a slight Russian accent.

"Yes?" Willoughby said curiously.

"My name is Nikolai Rostov," the voice replied. "I understand that you and your associates are facing a calamity in the realm of war and peace. I believe that I can help."

CHAPTER 6

Willoughby agreed to meet the Russian who offered to be his savior at the usual rooftop restaurant, which was proving ideal for confidential conversations, but his newly honed sense of drama and paranoia inspired him to take some preliminary precautions.

"Manny Slaughter!" Willoughby called out to his assistant in the next office.

"Yo!" Slaughter hollered back.

"What can you find out about Nikolai Rostov?"

"*Count* Rostov?"

"What?"

"Count Nikolai Rostov. He's one of the main characters in Tolstoy's *War and Peace*."

Willoughby sighed and wondered if he'd been punked by a mischievous caller—"the realm of war and peace," indeed. "See if there's a *real, living* Russian, maybe some official or diplomat or oligarch, who goes by that name."

He got up and walked to the doorway of Slaughter's office. His primo assistant was midway through his regular afternoon snack of a Diet Coke and a candy bar. Willoughby had once observed out loud that the calories foregone by drinking a Diet Coke were more than made up by the Snickers or Kit-Kat or Baby Ruth or whatever his munch du jour happened to be. Slaughter explained that his metabolism needed the daily jolt of caffeine *and* candy; the marketplace offered him a zero-calorie option for the former but not for the latter, so he had no choice.

Made sense.

"Hmmm, it's taking me a little while to get into the Cyrillic websites." Manny Slaughter mumbled while typing furiously on his laptop and peering at the screen over the black-framed glasses perched on his nose. After a half minute, he sat back in triumph. "Here he is: Nikolai Lvovich Rostov!" He scanned the obscure bio page, lips moving. "Seems to be a mid-level oligarch, a manager-turned-owner of a large timber forest, former higher-up in some unspecified security agency in St. Petersburg."

"Good. Thanks." At least the guy might not be some lunatic who fantasized an alt-life in a Russian literary classic. "Donna Cappella," he said, approaching his secretary's desk, "how would you like to take part in an adventure?"

"You want me to go to another seminar at the Brookings Institution and take notes?" she asked drily.

He'd given her several out-of-the-office tasks over the many months of her employment, to spice up moments when she seemed bored, though, yes, he had to admit, the recent Brookings brunch where he'd sent her—a roundtable discussion on the future of the Military Transport Command, which he couldn't attend—probably wasn't the liveliest of assignments. (She did take excellent notes on the talk, nonetheless.)

"No, this might be more fun. Certainly the food will be better."

He asked her to make two sets of dinner reservations: one for himself and a guest at 7:00, the time he'd agreed to meet Rostov; the other, fifteen minutes earlier, for herself and any friend she wanted to bring along, at the company's expense.

"Ask for my table to be next to the window in the back and for yours to be against the side wall," he instructed. "Over the course of dinner, if you notice anyone paying unusual attention to me and my guest, take a picture of him, or her, with your phone. Pretend to be photographing the food or your friend, like you're out for a night on the town, but zoom in on the suspect. Then, after it's all over, email me the photos."

"A-OK, James Bond," she said, not letting up on the deadpan.

Willoughby arrived at the restaurant a few minutes before seven. Rostov was already at their table and rose to greet him. He seemed to be roughly Willoughby's age with the air of a Western businessman, dressed in a suit and tie that were respectable but not particularly elegant, designed, it seemed, to blend into a crowd.

"Thank you for meeting with me," Rostov said after they shook hands and sat down. "No doubt you ran a Google search on my name before coming here, and you're puzzled as to precisely who I am or how I can help you."

"That's a fair summary," Willoughby replied.

"You can check with your high-level intelligence associates to confirm what I'm about to tell you," Rostov began. "I am a member of a small circle of advisers to my president, a sort of intermediary between the community of oligarchs and the Kremlin. One thing I do is float ideas—some at my own instigation—that the government cannot be seen as endorsing, at least not for the moment. And that is what I propose to do with you this evening."

Willoughby was tempted to ask what any of this could possibly have to do with *him*, but he was curious to hear more, so he stayed mum, fearful that raising the question might lead Rostov to realize that he'd phoned the wrong person and walk away.

"I am here to tell you that this war, which your government is cooking up against China, is very much inimical to the interests of the Russian Federation," Rostov said in a very serious tone. "You may have assumed otherwise, and it is true that, on the one hand, we would very much like to see the USA and China severely weakened, which would be one result of this war. Our top priority in recent years has been the disruption of democratic institutions in your country and the severing of Washington's ties with its allies worldwide. However, I am among those—an increasingly large group in Kremlin councils—who believe that we have gone too far with this strategy. The masters of this strategy wanted to *control* the pace of your country's unraveling—an overly ambitious goal, I thought at the time—yet your politicians have taken matters down this path so rapidly that the string is practically snapped. There are few remaining levers for us, or for anyone, to pull."

Willoughby suppressed a smile. "I must say, Dr. Willoughby, we were—and remain—agog at just how badly your leaders have *screwed things up*." Rostov smiled, perhaps at his italicized mastery of American jargon and, satisfied with himself, dialed up the haughtiness "It astonishes us that you have declared war—if not actual war, then political or economic war—against both the Russian Federation and the People's Republic of China You no longer have the power to influence or command others unilaterally, yet this is what you are trying to do. Now you're plunging into a shooting war with China right along their coastline, where they are strongest and you are weakest—so much so that, as you know more than most, the USA may very well lose. At that point, the entire Indo-Pacific region, as you now call it, will come under Chinese control—and that will severely erode the power of *our* government, as well as yours, not just geopolitically but probably in our domestic politics too."

The waiter approached, and the two ordered. Willoughby took the opportunity to glance over at Donna Cappella, who was sitting with a female friend and taking pictures of somebody. When the waiter left, Rostov continued.

"I am among those—initially quite a small group but now growing in number—who believe that it was always a mistake, first for you and later for us, to 'engage' with Beijing. Their rulers, beginning with Mao, have always been what we call 'revisionists'—they would never be satisfied to be a mere player, even a major player, in a system created by others, whether it was the world communist system that we wanted them to join under Moscow's oversight in the fifties and sixties or the Western financial system that Richard Nixon and Henry Kissinger hoped they would join in the seventies.

"And by the way," he added, as if posting a footnote, "perhaps you can inform me, at some point, why your ruling circles continue to regard Kissinger as such a sage. He masterminded Nixon's trip to China, in large part, to pursue a policy of 'triangulation' against Moscow and to exert leverage in Indochina, but it had no impact either on our policies or on the course of the Vietnam War, which you proceeded to lose catastrophically. And, of course, we needn't get into his horrid human-rights abuses, which, among other things, undermined your propaganda against *our* human-rights abuses."

Willoughby too had often puzzled over Kissinger's renown, but again he kept quiet.

"Anyway," Rostov went on, returning to his main theme, "the Chinese are out for domination on their own terms, and their terms have a very long horizon. You may recall that, during his historic trip to China, Kissinger asked Chou En-lai whether he thought the

French Revolution had been a mistake, and Chou En-lai replied, 'It's too soon to tell.' I don't know if that's a true story, I'm told it isn't, it sounds like something Kissinger would make up—he was, if nothing else, a witty man—but it *rings* true, it is consistent with how Chou En-lai and Mao Zedong thought, and with how the current leaders think as well."

The waiter came to the table with wine and poured a taste into Willoughby's glass. He swirled it, took a sip, and nodded his head. The waiter poured more into both tumblers, then left, though not before Willoughby noticed Donna Cappella snapping still more photographs.

"There was a time, back in the sixties," Rostov went on, "when Brezhnev contemplated invading China up to the Yalu River, but he held back, fearing that Mao might retaliate with his handful of atomic weapons—and he might *have*, Mao was *that* crazy. But I am among those who think, in retrospect, that maybe Brezhnev should have gone ahead with his plan anyway. Well, we now have a chance to replay history."

He paused, as if waiting for a response.

"What are you proposing—that Russia invade China?" Willoughby asked, incredulously.

"Not quite," Rostov said with a slight chuckle. "But I am proposing a grand historical reversal on many fronts, a restoration of what our respective leaders should have pursued all along—a Russian-American alliance against China. In this ongoing crisis, if Moscow were to (a) mobilize ground, air, and naval forces in the Vladivostok district on our eastern border with China, (b) put the squeeze on Chinese development projects in central Asia, (c) elevate our nuclear alert, and (d) signal our intention to respond with force to any attempt by Beijing to destabilize the region, I believe the Chinese would back off."

Rostov paused, but Willoughby's head was spinning too wildly to fashion a reply.

"Look," Rostov said, as if reading all too clearly his dinner companion's bewildered expression, "the era of the Cold War, when Washington and Moscow ruled our respective spheres of the globe, was far more peaceful and stable than the mad anarchy that rages now."

"Well," Willoughby said, managing to clear his throat enough for a rejoinder, "there *was* the Cuban missile crisis and a few almost-wars over Berlin."

"*Pshhht,*" Rostov replied, waving his hand dismissively. "Those were Khrushchev's harebrained schemes. In the sixty years since then, there have been no such direct confrontations between our two militaries—*none,* in *sixty* years! Meanwhile, you have crossed the Rubicon of *direct* conflict—your armed forces versus their armed forces—with China, a nuclear power that is much stronger than the Soviet Union was in 1962."

"What about your annexation of Crimea and your invasion of Ukraine?" Willoughby countered.

"You disappoint me, Dr. Willoughby," Rostov replied. "Crimea has always been part of Russia, and everybody knows it. Yes, Khrushchev transferred it to Ukraine in 1954 as a gift, but Russia and Ukraine were both part of the Soviet Union, which was the operative power, so the gift was purely symbolic. And Ukraine itself—I was in Moscow in the early nineties, when Yeltsin let American economists come in and try to turn the place into a new capitalist paradise. Billboards went up all along the Ring Road—billboards *in English.* I was fluent in English, but even to me, it felt as if my homeland was being invaded. We couldn't do anything about it. We were flat on our backs, our economy in disarray, our military wrecked. Your President Clinton assured Yeltsin that he would not expand NATO, then did just that, absorbing nearly all of our former Warsaw Pact allies into the Western military alliance. Later, when his wife, as Obama's secretary of state, encouraged Ukraine to join the European Union, even saying she would consider its application to join NATO, we had no choice. Ukraine was the buffer between Russia and all conquerors from the west—and, besides, it had been *part* of Russia for hundreds of years. We could not let that threat stand."

Willoughby was outraged by this distortion of history and blithe excuse for an act of imperial aggression, but he had no desire to turn the dinner into an argument, so he moved on. "What about your interfering with our elections?" he managed to say. "Why would any American president want to join an alliance—why would the American people let him join an alliance—with a country that's bent on subverting our democracy?"

"As I acknowledged, we went too far," Rostov said. "We underestimated just how ripe your people were for political disintegration. We are ready to make amends on that front. Look, Dr. Willoughby—Serge, if I may—your people and my people have a great deal in common. We were allies in the Second World War. When have you ever been allies with China? We jointly developed a vaccine against smallpox. Look at how Chinese duplicity spread pandemics worldwide. Look at our cultures. The Russians of my generation love American rock 'n' roll and jazz—your music helped inspire our second revolution. Thousands of American musicians to this day learn to play Prokofiev and Rachmaninoff. You read Tolstoy and Dostoevsky. We read Mark Twain and Faulkner. Does anyone in your country yearn to prattle on the one-string violin that the Chinese beggar from Queens bows on the New York subway platforms? Does anyone in your country or mine read Chinese literature?"

Willoughby felt he'd heard the full pitch by now, so he asked the question foremost in his mind. "This is all very… *interesting*, but what do I have to do with any of this? Why are you bringing this to me? Shouldn't someone from your foreign ministry be talking about this with someone in my State Department?"

Rostov laughed. "As I said, this is the sort of thing that cannot be discussed on an official level without first testing it through powerful but informal intermediaries. And each of us, in our own ways, is a velikii kombinator, as we say in Russian—a great operator, a big shot."

Now it was Willoughby's turn to laugh. "But I'm just a consultant. I'm not *any* sort of shot, much less a *big* shot. I'm way below the level of an informal channel to real power."

Rostov cocked an eyebrow in skepticism. "You are being far too modest. We both know that you are a *central* figure in this buildup to war. First, you make a phone call that incriminates Wolf Mandelbaum and sabotages a peace overture between certain American and Chinese diplomats. Then you meet inside the Pentagon with the secretary of defense and the chairman of the Joint Chiefs of Staff. Then, the next morning, you have breakfast with the director of the Central Intelligence Agency."

Willoughby sat frozen.

"We're not quite sure what game you're playing," Rostov went on, "but your intimate connections with both sides of the America war policy machine have led us to conclude that you are *the* person to reach out to. Are we wrong?"

Willoughby didn't know how to respond. At this point the waiter delivered their main courses, which gave him a few seconds to ponder his next move. Should he straighten out Rostov on his misunderstanding, which the Kremlin leadership apparently shared? Or should he let the illusion stand and somehow use it as leverage to stop the war? Clearly, either way, he was now in way over his head. He would have to consult with Danica Bloom; and to do that, he would—finally—have to confess everything about the call from Mandelbaum's telephone. Meanwhile, he needed to resolve one mystery. "How do you know about all this?"

Rostov chuckled. "You answered the question yourself with your denunciation of our activities in your elections. We are very good at wiretapping and hacking. Quite honestly, it is almost the only thing that we are very good at."

Walking home, Willoughby checked his phone for email. Donna Cappella had sent him a dozen pictures of two men who were gazing intently at his table. One, who appeared to be Asian, he didn't recognize, but the other, stocky, with a severe comb-over, seemed familiar. He enlarged the image and squinted at the facial features. He couldn't be certain, but it looked like one of Danica Bloom's security goons from their breakfast.

As he entered his apartment building, the doorman called his name. "A messenger delivered this package for you just a few minutes ago."

Willoughby thanked him and, walking toward the elevator, opened the manila envelope. It contained a cell phone and a note. It read:

> Turn on the phone. Tap ###. Hang up. I will call you. DB.

After entering his apartment and locking the door behind him, he poured himself a stiff drink, sat down in his favorite chair, and did as he was told. A few seconds later, the phone rang. He answered it.

Of course, it was Bloom, and she was fuming.

"Serge," she said, "what the *fuck* were you doing, having dinner with Nikolai Rostov?"

"Are you following him or me?" Willoughby replied as suavely as he could manage.

"I'm on the verge of throwing the book at both of you," she shot back, having none of his stab at playful repartee. "He's in the country illegally. By consorting with him, you're at the very least complicit to whatever he's cooking up. Now what's going on?"

"He proposed—he *says* on behalf of the Kremlin leadership—the cockamamie idea of a Russian-American alliance to divide the globe in two, just like in the good old days of the Cold War, which he says will stop Chinese aggression in the short run and make the world a more orderly place in the long run."

"Why would he bring this idea to you?" Bloom asked, derisively.

"That's what I asked. He insisted that I am obviously at the center of American war policy, citing as evidence my high-level meeting in the Pentagon and my breakfast with you. And there was one other thing, which I need to tell you about now."

"Oy," Bloom sighed, "there's more?"

"I was the one who made the call from Wolf Mandelbaum's phone the other night," he said, trying to maintain a calm, even tone. "I was pissed at him about a lot of things, I wanted to puncture his arrogant bubble, toss him a scare. I had no idea he'd be arrested. I obviously knew nothing about the back channel to China."

He paused, waiting for a response. Bloom was breathing erratically. It sounded like her head were about to explode.

"Rostov knows that I made the phone call," he went on. "When I asked him how he knew, he said that Russia is very good at wiretapping and hacking, that they're almost the only thing it's very good at."

Bloom sighed. "You have no idea what you've unleashed," she said, more in despair than in fury. "Look, I didn't want to tell you this. The *Chinese* are also very good at hacking and tapping, and their people in the back channel think that you're a central figure in our policy too. They don't know about the call from Wolf's phone—they don't know anything about our discovery of their hardware store spy network—but they do know about your two studies on war with China, the one that's forming the basis of our war plan *and* the one that argues against war. They know about your briefing with the top officials at the Pentagon, and they know about your breakfast with me. From all this, they infer that you're the guy making it all happen, negotiating with all factions. In any case, they don't trust me anymore, they certainly don't trust the White House or the Pentagon. So, they want to negotiate with you."

Willoughby was swilling some Scotch around in his mouth, and at Bloom's final words, he spit it out in a geyser, like a comic in a vaudeville routine.

"You're deep in the shit now," she went on, thoroughly agitated. "We have no choice but to bring you in and pretend that the Chinese—and, now you tell me, the Russians—are right about who you are." She added, with bitter sarcasm, "The fate of the world depends on you, Serge Willoughby."

Oh, Christ, Willoughby thought. *The whole fucking world is deep in the shit.*

CHAPTER 7

At 7:00 the next morning, the phone rang. It was Bloom.

"How come you're calling me on my landline?" Willoughby asked.

"Good news," she replied, "which means, among other things, we no longer need the encrypted burn phones. I've been up all night, on the phone and writing emails. I think I've straightened this whole thing out. I told Secretary Portis that we have very reliable intelligence that Mandelbaum did not make the phone call, that one of his houseguests did, and that I need him to order an NSA technician to compare the raw tapes from that call with some other recording of Wolf's voice. He did it, and word came back—from a more thorough analysis than your contact was able to conduct—that Wolf did *not* make that call. By the way, I did not tell him who did make the call, and he doesn't care who did, though the FBI might at some point. Anyway, Portis now accepts that Wolf is not a Chinese spy and that, therefore, the peace initiative was legitimate."

Willoughby slumped in his chair, relieved that this absurd nightmare was ending.

"Then," she went on, "I told my back channel in China's UN mission that Wolf had been arrested by militarists who want to sabotage the peace initiative and that he was about to be set free, so the peace talks are back on. I think I persuaded him, but he's waiting to see a dated photo of Wolf back on the streets and a news story about some Pentagon higher-up getting fired. Anyway, in the meantime, he said he could get his bosses to agree to a cease-fire. So…"

Willoughby heard panicked whispering on Bloom's end of the call. "*What?!*" she hollered to someone else in her office. Several seconds passed. Willoughby tensed up and bit a few fingernails, a habit he'd kicked long ago. "Goddammit," she moaned, coming back on the line. "The Chinese fired two missiles at one of our aircraft carriers. It isn't sinking, but a big piece of the deck is on fire, a few planes blew up, probably a hundred of the crew are dead or seriously wounded. In response, one of our Marine expedition units has occupied one of those militarized islands in the South China Sea." She sighed. "This thing isn't over yet."

"What do you think it means?" Willoughby asked.

"Maybe those operations were in the works before my contact got word to Beijing. More likely, though, it's just the dynamics of escalation at work. Our defense secretary may know that Wolf Mandelbaum isn't a Chinese spy, the Chinese defense minister may know that the peace initiative had nothing to do with Wolf's arrest—but it's too late. The conflict is running on its own momentum, independent of how it started."

"It's like the Gulf of Tonkin resolution," Willoughby reflected. "Everyone knew after a while that the North Vietnamese *didn't* attack one of our ships in Tonkin Gulf, but by that time, Lyndon Johnson had stepped up our intervention and the war was on."

"Yeah, something like that," Bloom replied. "If this goes on for years or kills tens of thousands of people, your fucking phone prank will go down in history as the Tonkin Gulf of the US-China war."

An hour later, during his walk to work, Willoughby sent a message to the AOL account that he and Chas were using as a private chat channel.

Was that you doing the early morning voice analysis?

Five minutes later, he received a reply:

Yes (★yawwwn★). Confidence-level still wasn't 100%, but I said it was.

Willoughby wrote back:

Figured. Thanks.

By this time, Willoughby had entered the lobby of his office building and stepped into the elevator. Three other people stepped in with him, all of them riveted to the morning's *Washington Post*, its large-font front-page headline blaring, "WAR IN THE PACIFIC: THE GATHERING STORM."

After a grimly quiet ride up, the elevator opened at his floor. He stepped out and opened the door to his reception area. Uncharacteristically, Donna Cappella wasn't at her desk. He heard the garbled audio of a cable newscast down the hall and walked to the conference room, where he saw all three of his staffers—Donna Cappella, Manny Slaughter, and Gupta—staring at the television, which he'd long ago bought for the office precisely to monitor crises, so he wasn't surprised that the set was turned on.

But he was surprised by what was grabbing the staff's attention. It was something that he hadn't seen—anywhere—for decades: a map of Washington DC and the surrounding area, overlaid with three circles. Willoughby recognized them as "bomb-damage circles," a commonplace in his grad school days, when nuclear war scenarios dominated defense studies, but he guessed that even devotees like his two research assistants were too young to have seen this before.

The camera cut to a burly man with a crew cut and a bad suit over a barrel chest who was explaining the meaning of the circles while holding a wooden pointer. He was no doubt a retired officer, probably one of the many colonels or one-star generals recruited by the news networks to comment on crises. He was an unfamiliar face, but this was an unfamiliar crisis.

"This inner circle represents the zone of prompt fatalities," the expert guest harrumphed.

"What exactly does that mean, general?" the host, who spoke in the tones of a Top Forty radio DJ, asked with undisguised nervousness.

The general looked at the host, then at the camera, then back at the host, this time with a sneer. Willoughby recognized the expression from the few times he'd watched a military officer, especially one high up in nuclear war commands dealing with uncleared civilians who had no idea of the shit about to come their way if (as such officers put it in their banal idea of a metaphor) "the balloon goes up."

"It means," the guest replied, "that if the Chinese attack the nation's capital with the type of nuclear weapons they're likely to use against such a key strategic target, then fifty to seventy-five percent of the people inside this inner circle will die right away, from either the blast of the explosion or the heat of the fireball."

"That circle covers almost half of Washington DC!" the host exclaimed.

"Yes, that's right," the general said, as if complimenting a slow school student on his sudden display of acumen. "Within the second circle," he droned on, moving the pointer outward, "fifty percent will likely die some hours or days later, from burns or radiation. In the outermost circle, which extends well into the suburbs, about fifty percent will die within a month from radioactive fallout."

"Is this guy on the level?" Donna Cappella asked in a voice pitched half an octave higher than usual.

Manny Slaughter and Gupta were both flailing away at their handheld calculators.

"Yes," Gupta said, "he's pretty much right."

"Give or take twenty percent, depending on the winds," Manny Slaughter added, in a show of one-upmanship.

"Plus or minus another twenty percent, depending on whether the warhead is airburst or groundburst," Gupta said, as if laying down a trump card.

Willoughby watched this exchange with an eerie nostalgia, recalling his grad school days, when he too cultivated the pose of a cool savant staring fearlessly into the thermonuclear abyss. The taunt was theoretical back then; it seemed unnervingly plausible now.

"You guys," Donna Cappella sighed, unamused, a proper response, Willoughby mused, as she walked back to her desk.

Willoughby turned toward the doorway as well, but Gupta stopped him, holding out his notepad, no doubt filled with jottings on the war's recent developments. "Substantial escalation in the overnights," he began in a solemn tone.

"I know all about the aircraft carrier and the island occupation," Willoughby said preemptively.

"Even before those incidents."

"I saw some of that, too," Willoughby replied wearily, having spent more time than usual watching the cable news channels. "Sure, let's go over them."

Gupta ticked off the incidents, which he had recorded meticulously in his notepad:

Two American B-52 bombers dropped several dozen mines in the Taiwan Strait.

Chinese antiaircraft missiles shot down one of the B-52s while it was unloading.

One of the mines, landing close to the port, blew up a Chinese troop-carrying ferryboat, killing at least fifty of their marines onboard.

Soon after, two Chinese missiles cratered a Taiwanese air base, destroying six fighter jets and killing at least a dozen crewmen.

A Chinese cruise missile slammed into the hull of a US Burke-class destroyer ship, killing thirty of the three hundred sailors onboard.

An hour later, an American P-3 Orion plane attacked and sank two Chinese diesel-electric submarines that were trolling American ships in the South China Sea.

Three US reconnaissance satellites, hovering over the area, suddenly malfunctioned.

North Korea launched two more ballistic missiles toward Japan. Just as they entered Japanese airspace, the Pentagon's command center, which was monitoring the test, lost all communications, possibly as the result of a Chinese cyberattack.

By the time IT specialists got the gear back online, four minutes later, the Japanese had fired a missile at a ship in North Korea's harbor, setting it ablaze.

"Adopting the terms of your study," Gupta concluded, "I'd say both sides are moving into escalation-dominance strategies."

He was right. Things were careening into chaos. Both sides might have thought they were playing a game of "*controlled* escalation," but as Willoughby knew from reading real-life histories, as distinct from academic theories, human beings—including political and military leaders—were rarely able to keep violence controlled once blood began to flow.

"You might also want to look at the new edition of *The Gold Mine*," Gupta said.

Ah, *The Gold Mine*, Willoughby thought. He hadn't heard from Natalie Gold in the last couple days. He opened her web page. There, in greater detail (and finer prose), was everything Gupta had just briefed him on, plus a couple of new tidbits. Willoughby read and reread one passage in particular:

> In recent weeks, Air Force and Navy officers have revised the results of simulated war games between the United States and China.
>
> Every such game in the last few years has shown China winning a war fought over control of Taiwan or the South China Sea.
>
> However, the revised games, supposedly based on new data concerning the capabilities of improved US weapons systems, show the United States winning.
>
> Meanwhile, sources tell *The Gold Mine* that, yesterday, Secretary of Defense Portis asked aides for a copy of an analytical study, commissioned three years ago by the Marine Corps, predicting a catastrophic defeat for US forces in a war with China. But apparently all copies of that report have disappeared.

If Gold was still aiming not merely to report the news but to "save the world," as she'd told Willoughby a few nights earlier in his apartment, this story was sending up some interesting flares. She was telling her Chinese readers, if there were any, that the US might have a shot at winning this war and that, therefore, they should think about backing off. She was signaling her friend Danica Bloom that James Weed Portis, the CIA's bureaucratic foe at the Pentagon, might be harboring doubts about these optimistic new war games and, with them, the advice he was hearing from his top generals and admirals—that, in short, Bloom had a shot at flipping the secretary of defense to her side of the bureaucratic war. (Gold probably wrote her story before Bloom's own wee-hours chat with Portis.) And she was informing Serge Willoughby that Portis, who'd held him in such contempt just a few days ago, was now looking for—was eager to peruse—his pessimistic study; that Willoughby, therefore, might have another crack at influencing the Pentagon's top civilian; that, as Bloom had told him in a different context and with considerable regret, he was in the game.

The phone rang. Willoughby picked up the receiver.

"Young Willoughby?" said the voice on the other end. It was Giles Molloy. "Meet me at the Tune Inn as soon as possible."

"It's a busy morning, Giles. What's this about?"

"Redemption, my friend," Molloy replied. "Remorse and redemption at the scene of the crime."

Willoughby hadn't been in the Tune Inn for years, maybe not for a decade. The owners had spruced the place up a bit—the floors were polished instead of coated with sawdust—but it otherwise looked like the grimy hole-in-the-wall of yore. He saw Molloy sitting in a booth, possibly (he couldn't be sure) the same booth where they'd sat and altered the course of Willoughby's life forty years earlier. As was customary these past several years, Molloy looked a bit spruced up too: a nice suit instead of a seersucker jacket with chinos, a leather fedora at his side instead of a Panama straw hat, custom shoes instead of loafers. ("I prefer fifty-dollar loafers," he once told Willoughby, "but my bunions prefer seven-hundred-dollar custom shoes.")

They greeted each other warmly. "Did you read Natalie Gold's newsletter today?" Molloy asked.

"Yes."

"Did you read the bit about the revised war games?"

"Yes, I thought that was… peculiar."

"I know all about that," Molloy said, "and I need you to put me in touch with Ike Douglass. Does he still owe you a big favor?"

"I used that up, but I think I still have some access," Willoughby replied. "What's going on?"

Molloy settled into his chair. "In the last year or so, I've been doing critical analyses of war games. You know the drill: there's the Blue Team, which plays us, and the Red Team, which plays the enemy. Well, I learned a while back that, when the Red Team wins, a lot of our officers get upset. They don't like word to get around— to the other officers, Congress, the president, or the real-life enemy—that we might lose the next war because they've done a shitty job running their little slice of the military budget. So, I came up with an angle: I would examine the assumptions of the game itself—see if the people who set the rules of the game had exaggerated the Red Team's strengths or the Blue Team's weaknesses. It's been a good sideline, it's pretty easy, and sometimes, it's turned out, the games really were stacked against the Blue Team."

A waiter came over. It wasn't quite 10:30 in the morning, but Molloy ordered a Scotch and a beer along with his usual onion rings. Willoughby asked for a cup of coffee.

"Well, a few months ago," Molloy went on, "I got a call from the chairman of the Joint Chiefs of Staff, you know, that Air Force prick, General Montgomery Vollmer." Molloy stretched the syllables of his name with mock arrogance. "He wanted me to take a close look at the war games of the last three years showing that we get our asses kicked in a quick, no-warning war with China. I did the job, really examined the games carefully, spent a week or so, nonstop, checking all the assumptions, playing and replaying them, and I concluded that the games were on the level—the outcomes were fair. Vollmer says 'Thank you very much,' signs my invoice, another day at the office."

The waiter brought the drinks. Willoughby was intrigued, not only by the nature of the war game but by the fact that Molloy— who, he'd thought, had retired—was still deeply in the business.

"Then," Molloy went on, "I read in today's issue of *The Gold Mine* that the China war games have been revised, based on 'new data' about how great our latest weapons systems are, and, this time," we win—all this in the backdrop of a war erupting with China for real."

Molloy took a couple sips from each glass. "Needless to say, I didn't see any 'new data' that would have suggested any such outcome. Now I read that Portis is trying to hunt down the Marine Corps study concluding that we *lose* a China war, big time. That was your study, I assume, the one from a few years ago that critiqued the report you did a bit earlier for the Air Force and Navy?"

Willoughby nodded.

"So, I'm figuring the chiefs have been handing Portis a load of crap, assuring him that we'll come out of this war smelling like roses, so let's charge the ramparts, full steam ahead."

The waiter brought the onion rings. Molloy picked up two, bit into them, and washed them down with another couple of sips.

"And I assume," he resumed his train of thought, "that Portis isn't completely convinced. Now, Portis strikes me as a smart guy, but he doesn't know anything about weapons or war, and your friend Douglass is an *Army* guy, meaning he knows a lot about *ground* combat, but he doesn't know enough about high-tech air and naval warfare to challenge what the chiefs are saying. So, I need to talk with Douglass, who I hope can bring me in to Portis, so we can stop this bullshit before a lot of people get killed and the world goes up in smoke."

"I think I can make that happen," Willoughby said. "But there's something I need to tell you." He paused for a few seconds, sighed, then told his old mentor the entire story of the last few days—the call from Mandelbaum's phone and how it disrupted peace talks and reignited tensions, his renewed contact with Danica Bloom, the dinner with the Russian, the interest in a meeting from the Chinese. "Now I'm in the thick of it," he concluded. "The foreign players think I'm a major dude, so, in a strenuous bid to stave off war, I've become one."

Molloy sighed. "For crying out loud," he mumbled. "All this is my fault in a way. This is the other thing I wanted to talk with you about. I led you down the wrong path that evening forty years ago at this very table. I taught you to regard this whole business of national security as a joke. In some ways—in most ways, really—it *is* a joke, but it's not *just* a joke. Yet you've built a career, at my encouragement, treating it as if it were, and that's why you could even *think* about pulling that stunt from Wolf Mandelbaum's phone, much less actually pulling it off—because, to you, it's just another joke. And look where it's led us. Look where we're at now."

He nibbled at an onion ring and downed his scotch. "We've betrayed our principles—you, me, the whole world of consultants," Molloy went on. "Our political leaders snared the nation into two godforsaken wars, in Afghanistan, then Iraq. They weren't as catastrophic as this war is bound to be—they weren't *world* wars—but what did we do about it? We analyzed tactics and techniques. Some good came out of it. Your MRAP study saved hundreds of American lives, no question. But we skirted the big questions. By dint of our education, our experience, and our access to information, we were better placed than just about anybody to judge whether these wars were *necessary*, whether they served our *interests*, made us more or less *secure*. And we skipped out. We abrogated our responsibilities."

Willoughby's head started to spin, a wave of revulsion, laced with nostalgia, rolling through his consciousness. All week long he'd been smacked with moral censure and condemnation, from the town's best military journalist, then the secretary of defense, then the director of the CIA (who, compounding the intensity, was also an ex-girlfriend), and now one of his closest confidants and his most pivotal mentor. Clearly their blows were hitting a mark, taking their toll. How much, Willoughby wondered, would he have to unravel, not just to help stop the onrush of war but also to figure out his own next steps in life—if, given the possibility of global catastrophe, there still were some next steps to be had.

Molloy took another onion ring and a sip of his beer. "I'm holding myself accountable, don't get me wrong. This analysis of the China war games that Vollmer had me do—I knew what he wanted me to say, and if the data hadn't been so clear-cut the other way, if the Red Team's victory had been even a little bit suspect, I probably would have said, 'Yeah, the game is distorted, let's have a do-over.'

It wouldn't be the first time I leaned in the client's direction. And I would have been complicit in what's going on now. I dodged the bullet because the results were so clear and I guess I still had a few grams of integrity. Now I'm Saul on the road to Damascus: I see the light, I've got to tell the people in charge that Vollmer is pushing this phony revised war game as a rationale for going ahead with the real war because it shows we're going to win—just like he used your original report for the Air Force and Navy as a strategy for *how* to win—and it's all bullshit."

While Molloy was soliloquizing, Willoughby got a text on his phone. It was from Ike Douglass:

> The boss is undecided, leaning in your direction. Big
> meeting with the brass happening soon. Big decision
> to follow. Get over here now! - Ike

Willoughby showed Molloy the text. They flung some cash on the table, dashed to the door, and, out on the sidewalk, hailed a taxi. Willoughby texted Douglass:

> On my way. Bringing Giles Molloy—you may
> remember him, an old friend and fellow consultant.
> He has some inside info that might help seal the deal.

CHAPTER 8

The taxi pulled into the driveway of the Pentagon's River Entrance, and Willoughby saw Ike Douglass waiting to greet him and Molloy.

"The boss is in a snit," Douglass said as they got out of the cab and walked toward the steps. "General Vollmer and his staff are giving him the runaround, and there's nothing that pisses him off more."

As they walked into the building, Willoughby explained why he'd brought Molloy along. By the time he finished explaining, they were approaching Portis's office.

"The boss will want to hear this," Douglass said, knocking on the door, then escorting them inside.

"Gentlemen," Portis said, acknowledging their entrance but continuing to read a memo on his desk.

Douglass whispered in Portis's ear, presumably informing him who Molloy was and why he was there.

"So, Willoughby," Portis said sharply, setting down the memo and looking up. "I hesitated to call you back to my office, since, as I told you the last time, I don't much trust the way you do business. But I thought you handled yourself with a modicum of principle at your briefing the other day. You took a stand, you took some risks, you took some heat. And while I was dissuaded from your conclusions at the time, I've since had reason to suspect that you were right and that my top officers are *bamboozling* me."

"Glad to do anything I can to help," Willoughby replied.

"Two things have changed my thinking," Portis went on. "First, I got hold of the study you wrote for the Marines. All the copies had been pilfered from the official files, but some midgrade officer in the Corps who'd kept a copy heard that I was looking for one and handed it over. I read it this morning and found it very compelling.

"Second, and I guess you know something about this already, I received high-quality intelligence this morning—not intelligence, really, but indisputable *facts*—that the impetus for going to war was *bullshit*. We'd heard, from what *seemed* to be unassailable sources and methods, that our man running back-channel peace talks was a Chinese spy and that the talks were a ruse enabling Beijing to mobilize for war. Turns out, this was all a load of *crap*. The authorities *arrested* this innocent, well-intentioned man under false pretenses, which led the Chinese to believe that *we* were no longer interested in peace. As a result, tensions reignited—these tensions had been pretty hairy before all this began, much hairier than most people knew—and war erupted."

Portis twirled around in his armchair, striking a contemplative pose.

"You know, I learned a valuable lesson when I worked on Wall Street," Portis went on, indulging his tendency to view any crisis through the lens of his past life. "If I bought a stock and it turned out to be overvalued, I unloaded it, cut my losses, *right away*. No point wishing and hoping for some rising tide to lift all boats! *This* boat's not coming back! Put my money—and my clients' money—on some *other* boat!

"That's the way I'm looking at this fucking war right now. We're clobbering them, they're clobbering us, I have no idea where it's going, they don't seem to know where it's going either, and now my top generals and admirals are telling me they see a clear path to victory, paved with some newfangled technology. I saw this over and over on Wall Street, too."

Willoughby and Molloy looked at each other. Willoughby widened his eyes, as if to say, *"This guy sees the whole world as Wall Street writ large."* Molloy shrugged slightly and cocked an eyebrow as if to say, *"Yeah, but he's making a good point."*

"You know," Portis continued, "I almost got snookered into the financial crisis of 2008. These smart young men came into my office with their elaborate models and flowcharts, showing the huge profits to be made from credit default swaps and heavily leveraged mortgage-backed securities. And I almost fell for it. But then I realized I didn't understand a single thing they were jabbering on about. Nothing they said jibed with my years of experience in finance, so I didn't go down that road, and as a result, I probably— no, I *certainly*—saved my firm from bankruptcy."

Portis rose from his desk, locked his hands behind his back, and paced around the room. "What I'm hearing from Vollmer and his smart young colonels and one-stars, about how we can fight and win this war with China, reminds me a lot of what I was hearing back then on Wall Street. It doesn't make sense, it's all abstraction. But I don't have the experience in war and peace that I had in finance, so I don't know how to fire back or how to tell my president that these highly decorated military officers are full of shit. Ike thinks it's all a load of crap too, but he's retired Army, so all the Air Force and Navy guys think he's out of his element."

Portis went back to his desk and grabbed a handful of papers. "In five minutes, I'm due over at the Joint Chiefs of Staff's conference room—the Tank, they call it—to get briefed on the technological wonder that will make victory ours, or so I'm told, and I need both of you gentlemen to come with me and ask the right questions."

Willoughby was perplexed. "Mr. Secretary," he said, "we're honored that you've asked us to provide assistance and advice, but why? There are dozens, maybe hundreds of experts and scientists in this building who could help you on this."

"Oh, some of them will be at this meeting, but I don't trust any of them," Portis snapped. "I've talked with them. Either they're afraid to speak up, or they're in line with Vollmer and his crew."

Willoughby found this hard to believe. He glanced over at Douglass, who glanced back and nodded.

"Plus," Portis added, "I'm told that you've emerged as the trusted intermediary among certain international actors. I don't quite know how this happened, and I don't know if I quite like it, but if you're the way out of this goddamned war, then I guess I'm bringing you along."

The four of them—Portis, Douglass, Willoughby, and Molloy—walked into the Tank, a compact but impressive auditorium, a war room that some crafty interior decorators designed to *look* like a war room, decked out with outsized monitors and maps, reeking of crisis and urgency. Already seated were General Vollmer, the other chiefs of staff, and a handful of civilian assistant secretaries of defense. The military officers all rose. Portis took his seat, and they followed suit.

111

"See that Air Force colonel and Navy captain standing together?" Molloy whispered to Willoughby, nodding toward two officers fiddling with the technical controls at the briefing lectern. "They're the jokers who were trying to give me a hard time during my review of the war game. They must have helped Vollmer write the revision."

Willoughby took a look. They were the same officers who'd raised eyebrows at each other during his all-too-brief talk in Portis' office a few days earlier. "They've been taking the piss at me, too," he whispered back.

Vollmer stood. "Mr. Secretary, thank you for taking the time to attend our presentation." He spoke in a wheezy voice, which surprised Willoughby, who'd never heard the general talk before. "The chiefs and I are going to *demonstrate* new *breakthrough* technology that, if put in motion, can all but guarantee victory in our evolving conflict against the People's Republic of China."

One of the giant screens lit up. It displayed a map of the South China Sea and the Taiwan Strait dotted with various icons. "The blue dots are US and allied ships. The red dots are Chinese ships. The blue rectangles are US submarines. The red rectangles are Chinese submarines." He paused to let his audience take a full look. "This is not a simulation. This is a real-time portrait—not a snapshot but a moving picture—of the location of these vessels. And yes, the submarines are underwater. We have accomplished the feat, long thought impossible, of making the oceans transparent."

Molloy looked at Willoughby and rolled his eyes. "They mentioned no such thing during the war game review three weeks ago," he whispered.

Willoughby scribbled some notes and passed them to Douglass, who was seated to his right. Douglass took a look and passed them on to his boss. Portis read them slowly, looking up now and then to catch Vollmer's eye and to scan the screen.

"On your order," Vollmer went on, "we can disable or destroy every single one of these Chinese ships and submarines in a matter of five minutes—ten, tops. We can, in short, take out their entire navy—and, of course, their air and ground installations, if we choose—before they know what's hit them."

Vollmer sat down with an air of command and confidence.

"Thank you, Monty," Portis said. "I do have some questions. First, what is the new technology that's enabled us to accomplish this amazing feat?"

"I'm afraid I can't go into detail on this, since some of the attendants lack the requisite security clearances," Vollmer said, glaring at Willoughby and Molloy. "But I can say it's related to a new satellite that we've launched in the last several months."

"My comptroller is sitting right over there," Portis said, pointing to a civilian wearing thick glasses and a striped tie. "Would you kindly have one of your aides give him the satellite program's reference code, so he can look it up in one of those big books that he brought along?"

"Yes, sir."

Portis paused as if to wait. "I mean, have one of your aides give him the code *right now.*"

"*Yes*, sir," Vollmer replied. He directed one of his aides to go give the code to the comptroller.

"Now you say the satellite was launched in the last several months," Portis said, resuming his cross-examination. "Mr. Molloy?" He turned to his side to address the guest. "You reviewed a highly classified US-China war game recently. When was that?"

"Three weeks ago, Mr. Secretary."

"Three *weeks* ago," Portis repeated. "Did a satellite with these sorts of capabilities play any role in that game? Was the existence of such a satellite even mentioned?"

"No, sir."

"Mr. Secretary," Vollmer interjected. "The satellite system experienced a breakthrough in its operational tests just *two-and-a-half* weeks ago."

By this time, the comptroller was flipping through one of his doorstop-sized books, looking for the satellite program. He found the page, then read it to himself quickly, moving his lips. "Mr. Secretary," the comptroller said, still reading. "This budget book is updated weekly, and it says this particular satellite system hasn't had any *operational* tests. It's still undergoing *development* tests of its individual components."

Portis flashed one of his steel-glint looks at Vollmer.

"Mr. Secretary," the general said in a subdued tone, "I would rather discuss this in a more restricted setting."

"Let's do that, *right* after this meeting," Portis said. "Now, one more question about your map. Are you saying that all the dots and boxes on this map indicate *exactly* where these vessels are *right now*? Let's take that submarine of theirs that looks like it's out on the edge of the South China Sea"—he read aloud the latitude and longitude— "not very far from one of our aircraft carriers. If we were to fire a torpedo or drop a submergible bomb on that spot, the submarine would be *right there*? We would *definitely* hit the target?"

Vollmer nodded toward the Navy captain as a cue for him to elaborate.

"Mr. Secretary sir," the captain said, standing at attention, hands clasped behind his back. "The short answer is, yes, almost certainly."

"What's the *long* answer?" Portis asked with barely disguised contempt.

"Sir," the captain replied, "the images you see are derived from plotlines of where the submarine has been in the past several hours, minutes, and seconds. These plotlines are plugged into a stochastic model of the vessel's subsequent trajectory, computed through ten million rounds of Monte Carlo simulations, which are then correlated with signatures of actual objects in the vicinity—created by acoustical patterns, turbulent wakes, reflections of imagery, and so forth. With those correlations, we can nail down their identity and location with high confidence."

Willoughby knew this was precisely the sort of answer—packed with jargon, intended more to obscure than to clarify—that would really piss Portis off.

Portis stared the captain down. "I *do* know what a *stochastic model* is. The term originated in the financial business, where I've spent most of my life. It means *random*. Yes, I know it doesn't quite mean random the way most people use the term, but essentially, it's *random*."

Willoughby looked over at Vollmer, who was looking straight ahead, breathing a bit more heavily than he had been a moment before.

"So," Portis went on, "when you say that you know with *high confidence* that this dot is a submarine or a destroyer ship, how are you defining 'high confidence'—a ninety percent probability, eighty percent probability?"

"I would say ninety percent, sir," the captain replied.

"Ninety percent. And I assume that, quite apart from whatever calculation gave you this number, the whole predictive model has a p value of point-zero-five. right?" Portis asked.

"Yes, that's correct," the captain replied, apparently surprised, no doubt along with everyone else in the room, that Portis knew what a p value was. Actually, Portis probably didn't know what a p value was. He was clearly riffing off of Willoughby's notes, but he'd memorized them thoroughly and was reciting their bullet-points very naturally. Willoughby was impressed.

"So, let's do some math here," Portis reflected. "We start off with a ninety-five percent probability that this model is valid to begin with—that's what a p value of point-zero-five means. Then we multiply that by your ninety percent chance that the system is accurate on the objects' location. *Then* we factor in the kill-probability of our latest anti-submarine weapon—the chance that it destroys the target it's aimed at—which is... Dr. Willoughby, Mr. Molloy, do you know offhand what that is?"

"Sir," Molloy piped up. "In the Joint Chiefs' war game that I reviewed, the kill probability of that weapon was eighty-five percent."

"So," Portis said, glancing up, as if he were toting some numbers in his head, "we've got ninety-five percent multiplied by ninety percent multiplied by eighty-five percent—that comes to about seventy-two percent. So, all told, we have a seventy-two percent chance that our bomb sinks the Chinese submarine." He paused. "That's pretty good, but I wouldn't call the chances *almost certain*, as you did a few minutes ago, Captain."

The room fell silent.

Vollmer leapt in. "There is another factor to take into account. For that, I would like to turn the floor over to the director of special projects at US Cyber Command, Major General Manuel Ray, or, as his associates call him, X-Ray."

Willoughby strained to suppress his laughter. The Air Force had a way with nicknames. In his experience, every Air Force officer named Rhodes was nicknamed "Dusty," every Air Force officer named Campbell was nicknamed "Soup." But "X" for an officer named Ray—*that* was a new one. It was clever, since the phrase pretty much described what a special projects director at Cyber Command *did*: he looked through things (or tapped or hacked them), kind of like an X-ray.

Ray stood up. A short, white-haired Latino man with the hint of a grin, he looked serious but jovial, as these whimsically nicknamed officers tended to be. "I am going to show you something remarkable and not at all theoretical or probabilistic—this is *real*," he began, with what seemed to be a bit of a dig at the Navy captain's briefing, suggesting that *it* had not been quite real.

Willoughby glanced at Vollmer, who was on the verge of fuming.

Ray clicked a button, and a new image came up. It was a picture of a radar screen. "This is a Chinese army radar screen. *I'll* be honest." (Another dig at the Navy captain and Vollmer?) "It's not a Chinese radar screen at this very moment. It's an image that I captured on a thumb drive back at Fort Meade. But when I captured the image, earlier today, it was of a Chinese radar screen at *that* very moment. In other words, when this image was shot, I was looking at—a lot of our analysts were looking at—exactly what Chinese radar operators were looking at."

He paused to let that sink in. Portis looked sideways at Willoughby, as if seeking confirmation. Willoughby, who'd heard about this program, returned a slight nod.

"We've been able to do this," Ray went on, "with a lot of foreign military radar screens all over the world for a long time. Recently we have figured out how to do this with the integrated radar systems of the Chinese military.

"Now here's the thing about cyber operations," he went on. "Anything I can hack, I can manipulate. So not only can I see what the radar operator is seeing, I can *change* what he sees—I can alter, disrupt, or erase the image and put up a whole new image. One minute, he's looking at a sea full of ships or a sky full of fighter planes. The next minute, he's looking at a blank screen—nothing seems to be out there. Or some ships or planes seem to be over *here*—but actually they're over *there*."

Vollmer interrupted: "The point, Mr. Secretary, is that the system that X just described and the satellite system that we described earlier have a *synergistic effect*." Another phrase that Portis almost certainly detested. "Even if the satellite system is less than perfect, if we activate its sensors *and* hack the enemy's radar, so he doesn't see where we are or what we're doing, we can inflict devastating damage on his naval forces. As far as this war is concerned, it's a *game changer*." Yet one more cliché that, Willoughby suspected, Portis found irritating.

"Let me ask you this, General Ray," Portis said, looking past Vollmer, who must have noticed that the secretary had called him by the diminutive of his first name (*Monty*) but had addressed Ray, who had two fewer stars on his epaulette, as *General*. "Can the Chinese do the same thing to *our* radars? Are *we* vulnerable to the same sort of hack?"

"Sir," Ray replied, "we don't know whether China has the capability to hack our radar systems in precisely this fashion, but yes, our radars *are* vulnerable. In our war games, Red Teams hack into the Blue Teams' radar screens and erase targets, or superimpose spurious targets, all the time—I mean, in *every* war game where that is part of the scenario."

"So let me get this straight," Portis said. "If we hacked into China's radar and flicked on this satellite, assuming it works really well, then *maybe* we could sink their whole goddamn navy in short order. *Or* maybe they respond by screwing with *our* radar, and then we're both stumbling in the dark like two blind men in a warehouse full of tripwires and dynamite, firing missiles and dropping bombs on who-knows-what, probably doing a lot more damage than we otherwise would have, with no way of screeching this thing to a halt. Would you say that sums it up?"

"Yes, sir, I would say so," Ray said with a slight grin.

Willoughby glanced at Vollmer, who, even from ten feet away, could be heard grinding his teeth.

"So," Portis said, "what would you think of *this*, Monty?"

Vollmer ground his teeth so hard, it sounded like he broke a crown.

Portis went on. "What if I were to call my Chinese counterpart and tell him to have his commanders look at their radar screens. General Ray and his folks at Fort Meade make the screens go blank, then make them look like there's three times as many ships out in the sea or who knows what other tricks. Then I say, 'We can run you ragged like this for hours, days, weeks, months, while we sneak up behind you and destroy all your assets—*or* we can both agree to a ceasefire and work all this out in a less crazy fashion.'"

"The problem with that idea, Mr. Secretary," Vollmer grumbled, barely able to contain himself, "is that, once we show and tell the Chinese what we can do, they can devise countermeasures and workarounds, so their radars will be back up in no time."

"Is that so, General Ray?" Portis asked.

"It's possible," Ray replied, "but we haven't figured out how to do that in any of our war games. The vulnerability seems to be *inherent* to the systems, and the few times we've tried to deal with the problem, it's taken weeks, sometimes months, to reprogram the settings."

Portis nodded his head. "I think I've heard enough here." He turned to Douglass. "Ike, you and General Ray get on the phone with the head of Cyber Command when we get back to my office so we can get this demonstration underway."

He rose. The officers rose as well, Vollmer a bit shakily. Portis walked out with Douglass and Ray. Willoughby and Molloy followed.

Once Portis was out of the room, Vollmer grabbed the two consultants by their shoulders. "You don't know what damage you've done," he hissed at them. "This is the last chance that our nation can halt the Chinese juggernaut. Even if this *stock broker* persuades them to cease fire now, they'll keep building up, and in five years' time, there will be no stopping them. They'll take over the planet, the American empire will be in the shitter, and it will all be on *you* fucking idiots."

Willoughby looked around to see if anyone was overhearing this. It turned out that several people still in the room, civilians and officers, were listening intently, some with jaws wide. He was about to deliver some savage reply, but the more even-tempered Molloy stepped in.

"You may be right, general," he said, "but let's deal with one avoidable war at a time."

CHAPTER 9

The next thing Willoughby knew, he was hustled into the defense secretary's limousine, along with Portis, Douglass, and Ray, for the thirty-minute car ride up the Baltimore-Washington Parkway to Fort Meade, the joint headquarters of the NSA and Cyber Command.

He was pleased to be included, but wondered halfway into the trip whether he was wasting his time. Tailored Access Operations, the agency's elite hacker unit, where they were ultimately headed, was a mini-agency all its own. It was ensconced behind two combination-locked doors. No outsiders could get in, not even other NSA employees, unless they were expressly invited. Willoughby had a Top Secret clearance, but even getting an invitation to enter would require a much higher-level clearance than Top Secret.

The limo screeched into the Fort Meade driveway. The passengers unloaded. Willoughby found himself walking between Portis and Douglas, not just through the gates of the NSA but up the elevator and into the TAO's inner sanctum. He was astonished. What was going on? Was his friend Chas Greenway's continued access to secrets, despite his clearly drunken state, no anomaly? Had security at the National *Security* Agency gone to tatters? Or had Willoughby somehow become a true insider, as Nikolai Rostov suspected? For someone who never had much desire to be a deep insider, the sensation of being treated like one gave him an electrified thrill.

They were all led into a vast briefing room. Willoughby looked around in a state of wonder. It was like the Joint Chiefs of Staff's war room in the Pentagon but bigger, glitzier, with technological gizmos that Willoughby had never seen before; it was as if some NSA superspies had time-traveled a decade or two into the future and hauled back the most advanced stuff that could fit in the spaceship.

Portis was handed an ultra-secure phone. Someone had already dialed the number of China's minister of national defense. After some cordial greetings and reminiscences (the two men seemed to have met on a couple of occasions), Portis cleared his throat and got down to business.

"I'd like you to have your air-defense commander look at his central radar screen in five minutes," Portis said. There was silence, as, presumably, the minister called the commander. Tension zapped the air. Were they about to witness a prelude to the end of the war or a spike of escalation? Nobody could begin to guess.

Portis looked up. Apparently the minister was back on the line. "Your commander is looking now?" he asked. Portis then nodded toward X-Ray, who in turn signaled his own technical operators. They were all looking at a screen that matched—because the NSA had hacked into—the screen that the Chinese were watching at that moment. X-Ray's crew did their magic. The screen, which had displayed a dozen or so icons indicating the warships and submarines in the South Dhina Sea, went blank. Ten seconds later, the screen was crammed with four times as many objects. Then the screen went blank again. Finally it reverted to normal.

Portis cleared his throat. "This is what we can do to you for as long as it takes," he told his counterpart in a calm tone. "Meanwhile, we can clobber all of your forces, and you won't see us coming. Now, I'd rather not do this. I'd rather that we both come to our senses and stop this damn war before it careens out of control. Why don't you consult with your superiors and send me a peace offering in the next thirty minutes. I'll show it to my president, and we can go from there."

With that, Portis thanked X-Ray and his crew, then walked out the way they came in. Douglas was close behind, Willoughby nearing a trot, worried that he might be arrested once some alert guard realized the mistake of letting him in. But no one stopped him, and he dashed into the limo.

Twenty minutes later, on their way back to Washington, Portis got a phone call from the Chinese defense minister. He put the phone on speaker, so Douglass and Willoughby could hear.

The minister, speaking through a translator, proposed a four-phase peace plan. First, he said, both sides would declare an immediate ceasefire. Second, the United States would withdraw its Marines from the Chinese island that they'd occupied and pull all planes and warships back into "international waters"—as China defined the term, meaning far away not just from China's coast but also from its artificial militarized islands (which the US and other countries regarded as international waters). Third, China would return all its transport ships to their home ports and demobilize the troops onboard. Fourth, over the next six months, diplomats on both sides would negotiate formulas for war damage reparations.

Portis thanked the minister for his prompt response and said he would inform the president.

At this point, Willoughby noticed, to his surprise, that the limo had reached his own office building in DuPont Circle. Portis gave him an appreciative nod and pointed to the car door. Willoughby thanked him for the ride and quickly got out.

He entered his office still in a daze, uncertain how much of what he'd just seen and heard he could share with his staff—probably, if he behaved himself, none of it.

Almost instantly he got a phone call. It was Douglass, telling him that the president had called a National Security Council Principals' meeting in the White House Situation Room, to include all the cabinet secretaries, intelligence chiefs, and senior-most military officers. "Now," he added, "the boss wants to talk with you."

Portis came on the line. "The NSC meeting is happening in one hour. I want you to meet me at the Pentagon, so that you can ride with me and Ike to the White House together."

"I'm going to an NSC Principals' meeting?" Willoughby asked in a high, almost squeaky voice.

"No, I don't think I can get you into the meeting," Portis replied. "But Danica Bloom says some of the Chinese higher-ups need to be persuaded more firmly that you really are an inside player. So, it would look good if the cameras showed you accompanying me into the White House right before a national security meeting that's likely to be the most important of the year, if not the decade. Now, there's one more thing, and I'm going to put Ike back on to talk to you about that."

Douglass came back on the line. "This meeting is going to be the final showdown between the boss and General Vollmer over whether we go to war or take the offer of a ceasefire. I have intel from a friend on the Joint Staff that the general will be playing the Kennedy card."

"What's that?" Willoughby asked.

Douglass expressed surprise that Willoughby had never heard of it. "The president is a John F. Kennedy fanatic. This is something that all of his aides and cabinet people have learned. The best way to sell him on a program is to say that President Kennedy supported the same kind of program. I'm told that General Vollmer is going to invoke the Cuban Missile Crisis, tell the president that Khrushchev put forth a peace deal—something like the deal the Chinese are offering now—but that JFK rejected it."

"I'm pretty sure that's a load of bullshit," Willoughby said. "I recall reading somewhere that Khrushchev offered to withdraw his missiles from Cuba if Kennedy removed American missiles from Turkey, and Kennedy *took* the deal. This was done in secrecy, the deal wasn't revealed until many years later, though I don't remember the details."

"Do you know someone who does know the details and can lay them out clearly and concisely, with supporting evidence, in case it's challenged?"

"I think I might," Willoughby said. "I'll have the information with me when I meet you back at the Pentagon."

Willoughby hung up, then shouted, "Gupta! Manny Slaughter!"

His two assistants appeared in his doorway seconds later.

"Does either of you know a lot about the Cuban missile crisis?"

"I wrote my undergraduate honors thesis on crisis management during the Berlin and Cuban crises of 1961–62," Gupta replied.

"Give me the elevator pitch on how the Cuban crisis was settled."

"Elevator pitch?"

Kids these days, Willoughby thought. "Let's say you have a big idea," he explained. "You get in an elevator with a client. He's going to the forty-fourth floor. You have to sell him on the idea by the time you get there. To put it another way, you have one minute. Go."

Gupta outlined the resolution of the missile crisis with admirable concision—he was getting good at this job—confirming Willoughby's vague recollection and adding a spellbinding detail.

"None of Kennedy's advisers wanted him to take Khrushchev's deal," Gupta said. "All of them—not just the generals, but Robert McNamara, McGeorge Bundy, even JFK's brother Bobby—all urged him to reject the deal and to start bombing the Russian missile sites in Cuba. Only President Kennedy wanted to take the deal. And he did."

"That's great," Willoughby exclaimed, shouting with excitement. This was precisely the sort of story that would appeal to a president aspiring to be another JFK, his advisers' opinions be damned. "What's the evidence for this?"

"McNamara and the others wrote an essay for *Time* magazine in 1982, on the twentieth anniversary of the crisis, admitting that it was settled by this diplomatic compromise. There are also the tapes. Kennedy secretly recorded all the cabinet discussions over the thirteen days of the crisis. And those tapes show that Kennedy was the only one who favored taking Khrushchev's deal."

"Are those tapes readily accessible?"

"Yes, they've been on the JFK Library's website for decades."

"OK," Willoughby said. "Gupta, you write up what you've just told me. No longer than one page. Manny Slaughter, you dig up that *Time* magazine essay and a snippet of the tapes. Gupta, you tell him which snippet he should look for. Text me all three—the summary, the letter, and the snippet—in a half hour. I've got to go to the Pentagon. I'll get it while I'm over there."

He stopped and turned to Gupta. "Is what you've told me widely known? Is this the version that's in all the history books these days?"

"No. Most of the histories still regurgitate the myth perpetrated by Kennedy's aides in their memoirs—the idea that Kennedy faced down Khrushchev through force alone."

"They've ignored the *Time* essay and the tapes? Why is that?"

Gupta shrugged. "Beats me."

Willoughby took a taxi to the Pentagon. On his way there, Gupta and Manny Slaughter came through. He read the summary, skimmed the *Time* essay, and listened to the audio clip. They were all clear and compelling. He forwarded the file to Douglass, who was waiting for him when the taxi pulled up to the River Entrance.

"I meant to ask you," Willoughby said as they walked into the building. "Did General Vollmer ever come brief Secretary Portis on that ultra-secret satellite program? He claimed at the meeting in the Tank that there had been some huge testing breakthrough just in the past couple weeks that—"

"No," Douglass interrupted. "He never did, though the secretary asked him twice to come by. He's just a bullshitter, making up stuff to drag us into a war. He's a disgrace to his uniform. The boss is *livid*."

"Meanwhile," Willoughby said, "I sent you the material on the Cuban missile crisis."

Douglass looked at his phone as they walked into the anteroom of Portis' office and handed it to one of his aides. "Major, would you print out the attachments in this email? Make thirty copies of each."

Five minutes later, the major came back with the copies, all collated into blue folders. *The Pentagon!* Willoughby marveled: its officers and bureaucrats couldn't design weapons systems in time or on budget, and they couldn't fight wars very well, but damn, they were wizards when it came to churning out paperwork!

Just then, Portis came out of his office. "Let's go."

As they rode to the White House, he perused the materials, just as he'd done with Willoughby's jottings at the meeting in the Tank. He also listened to the audio clip through ear buds that Douglass handed him.

After finishing, he looked up and nodded. "Very impressive, Willoughby."

The car pulled into the White House driveway.

"Stick close to me," he said.

As anticipated, a dozen photographers and video crews, waiting off to the side, documented their entrance. If any Chinese officials or spies were watching cable news or later took a look at the still shots, they would see Serge Willoughby striding alongside the secretary of defense just outside the West Wing of the White House, as if he belonged there.

They walked into the building, at which point Willoughby figured he'd be told to go sit in the waiting room. But no one told him anything. He got caught up in the push of the crowd, and, before he knew it, in a startling reprise of what had happened earlier that day at the NSA, he was in the Situation Room. An aide directed him to one of the rickety wooden chairs along the back wall, where various second-tier officials were sitting, including Douglass, who motioned Willoughby to sit next to him.

Willoughby had never been in the Situation Room, nor had he aspired to any job that would land him there for whatever reason. It was smaller than he'd imagined and jammed with people. Seated around the table on cushy black armchairs were ten or so cabinet secretaries, most of whom he recognized. Portis sat to the left of the one empty seat, at the head of the table, where the president would presumably be sitting when the meeting got underway.

Danica Bloom, sitting near the head of the table, noticed Willoughby in a vaudevillian double take, then squinted at him with intense puzzlement. She pointed at him and whispered something to Portis, who sat next to her. Portis looked at him in wide-eyed surprise for a second, then chuckled and shrugged.

There was a buzz in the room, though Willoughby didn't know whether there was always a buzz before a meeting with the president or whether the people in the room knew that this particular meeting was special, that it could mean the difference between war and peace, that they were about to witness history in real time. Willoughby wasn't generally susceptible to buzzes, but he sensed one vibrating in his head too; he not only understood but *felt* the gravity of the moment.

The president entered the room, and Willoughby realized he had never seen him in person. He'd met just two presidents in all his years in Washington, and then only briefly, at social gatherings or political fundraisers where he'd been dragged by a client or a date. He was taller, and seemed older, than he looked on television. His hair, brown when he'd won the office a few years earlier, was sheer white. It happened to most presidents, Willoughby mused. What a nerve-racking job. Who would want the aggravation? Everyone in the room rose, then sat down when the commander-in-chief took his seat.

"Thank you all," the president began. "As you know, we have a matter of utmost, even existential urgency to discuss today—the most urgent matter that any president and cabinet ever have to weigh. I'm not the slightest bit interested in how our decisions today will affect the stock market or the polls or my chances of reelection. I'm interested only in what is best for our national security, the interests of our allies, and the stability of the world."

Willoughby couldn't tell whether the president meant these words or whether he was just saying them so that some aide who later leaked the gist of the meeting could recite them. Maybe both.

"So," the president continued, "anyone should feel free to speak up or ask questions, but for the most part, I want to hear from Secretary Portis and General Vollmer. General, do you want to begin?"

Vollmer was sitting opposite Portis, with a half-dozen uniformed officers sitting behind him. "Mr. President, distinguished cabinet secretaries," he began. "Along with the officers of Indo-Pacific Command and the Joint Staff, I have developed a plan for fighting and winning this war. It is more detailed than many of you would be interested to hear, so I will brief it to you, Mr. President, and a few others later today. For now, I would like to address the so-called *peace* proposal that the Chinese government has placed on the table. If accepted, it would not lead to peace but would merely postpone—and not by long—Beijing's plan for global domination and the decline of our own influence in Asia and, over time, throughout the world.

"China's proposal," he went on, "reminds me of the offer that Soviet Premier Nikita Khrushchev put on the table near the end of the Cuban missile crisis."

Willoughby looked around the room and saw a few officials and aides rolling their eyes or rubbing their foreheads. He also noticed that the president leaned forward with avid interest.

"Khrushchev said that he would remove the Soviet missiles from Cuba if Kennedy removed our missiles from Turkey," Vollmer continued. "But President Kennedy, in his wisdom, rejected the deal, concerned—again, correctly, I believe—that accepting it would severely weaken NATO, alienate our Turkish allies, and gravely erode our credibility in the world at a time in the Cold War when our credibility was vital to the survival of Western civilization. Instead, as his secretary of state, Dean Rusk, later put it, President Kennedy went eyeball to eyeball with the Soviets—and the Soviets blinked."

The president laughed and under his breath whispered, "Fascinating."

"President Kennedy had the upper hand in that crisis and thus saw no need to cave in to Khrushchev's self-aggrandizing scheme," Vollmer continued. "In the same way, we have the upper hand in this present crisis, and it would only weaken our stance, in the region and in the world, to cave in to China's similarly one-sided proposal. Thank you."

"Very thoughtful, General," the president said. "Mr. Secretary?"

Portis took a breath and shuffled his papers. "Mr. President, I have the highest regard for General Vollmer and his lifelong service to our nation. He has provided sage wisdom and advice throughout your term, and our nation is stronger for it." Portis seemed courteous, modest, respectful—a different man from the profane fount of supreme self-confidence that Willoughby had seen in small private forums or on his home turf.

"I also appreciate the invocation of history in any analysis of our present-day crises," Portis went on. "We can learn a great deal from the lessons of the past, and it's a shame those lessons are so infrequently plumbed."

Willoughby leaned in, waiting for the punch that he'd set Portis up to deliver.

"However, Mr. President, in this instance, and it *pains* me to say so," he continued, in a convincing simulation of a pained tone, "General Vollmer has been misled by inaccurate history. Yes, one or two of President Kennedy's most devoted aides later wrote books telling a story that they thought their beloved commander-in-chief would want them to tell." In a theatrical aside, he added: "I can't imagine anyone doing that today, can you, Mr. President?"

This prompted a guffaw from the president and some chuckles around the table.

"But the actual history—and we now have declassified documents, tape recordings, and other artifacts—reveals a very different picture. The fact is, President Kennedy *took* Khrushchev's deal. He did so on the condition that Khrushchev keep the deal secret, and a small group among his own people kept it secret too, for many years."

Portis opened up his blue folder. "I would like to read you a portion of an essay that a few of President Kennedy's top aides—McNamara, Bundy, Rusk, Sorensen, some others—published in *Time* magazine on September 27, 1982, as they approached the twentieth anniversary of the crisis."

He asked Douglass to pass around the blue folders containing the essay. "The essay reveals some *secret* lessons of the Cuban missile crisis that they felt they could reveal only all those many years later. I draw your attention to what they call 'the eighth lesson.' They note that, in public, President Kennedy agreed simply not to invade Cuba if Khrushchev withdrew his missiles. But then they write this."

Portis read aloud from the essay:

> "'The second and private assurance—communicated on the president's instruction by Robert Kennedy to Soviet Ambassador Anatoli Dobrynin on the evening of October 27—was that the president had determined that once the crisis was resolved, the American missiles then in Turkey would be removed.'"

Portis paused. Some gasps punctured the room.

"More fascinating still, Mr. President," Portis continued, "is something that Bundy, McNamara, and the others did *not* reveal in their essay. And that is, during the crisis, all of them had urged President Kennedy *not* to take Khrushchev's deal. The deal was presented on a Saturday, which turned out to be the final day of the crisis. The Joint Chiefs of Staff's plan was to start bombing the missile sites in Cuba the following Monday, dropping five hundred sorties' worth of bombs each day, for five days, followed by a land invasion of Cuba. Again, all of President Kennedy's advisers urged him to go ahead with the bombing and the invasion. If he took Khrushchev's deal, they warned, he would wreck NATO, alienate the Turks, and destroy our credibility in the world."

Willoughby looked around. A few of the officials seemed momentarily confused, as if not knowing where the story was going. He knew their expressions would change dramatically in a few seconds.

"As we learned much later," Portis went on, "President Kennedy secretly taped these discussions, along with many other conversations. Those tapes were declassified a few decades ago. Listen to what President Kennedy himself said in response to his advisers' protests. The audio quality isn't perfect, but Colonel Douglass gave you all transcripts when he was passing around the *Time* essay, so please follow along."

Before the meeting had gotten underway, Douglass had given the White House audio/video technician a thumb drive of the clipping from the Kennedy Library. He now signaled the technician to play the clip. John F. Kennedy's voice came wafting through the room's loudspeakers, like a ghost.

> "I'm just thinking about what we're going to have to do in a day or so—five hundred sorties, possibly an invasion, all because we wouldn't take missiles out of Turkey. And we all know how quickly everybody's courage goes when the blood starts to flow, and that's what's going to happen in NATO. The Soviets will grab Berlin and everybody's going to say, 'Well, this Khrushchev offer was a pretty good proposition.'"

Willoughby wasn't old enough to remember John F. Kennedy, but he'd seen documentary footage of his press conferences, where he sounded so calm, so assured, so cool. The Boston Brahmin voice on the tape sounded exactly the same as it did at those press conferences.

He looked around the room while the tape was playing. Everyone was riveted, following along with the transcript. Bloom could barely contain herself, beaming with joy. The president seemed positively giddy, fidgeting in his chair, smiling with delight. Everyone was absorbed except Vollmer, whose eyes bespoke pure misery and whose teeth were grinding another molar into dust.

Portis signaled for one more excerpt from the tape to be played, another remark by JFK after his aides warned him one more time not to take the deal. Again, the voice rang through the room

> "We can't very well invade Cuba with all its toil, and long as it's going to be, when we could have gotten them out by making a deal on the same missiles in Turkey. If that's part of the record, I don't see how we'll have a very good war."

"Wow," someone around the table exclaimed, while others whistled, sighed, or whispered among themselves.

"That was amazing," the president said.

"I can supply you—or anyone else—with the complete tapes and transcripts for that entire day, or for all thirteen days of the crisis, if you're interested," Portis said.

"I may take you up on that!" the president piped up. "What a privilege to hear this. And talk about the lessons of history! There's a rich trove just in those brief clips. Well, listen, I think that sums it up. Unless someone has something really important to say, I'm bringing this meeting to a close."

Douglass leaned over to Willoughby and whispered, "Game, set, and match."

"I think you owe me another big favor," Willoughby replied.

CHAPTER 10

Willoughby walked the mile from the White House to his office, strolling through Lafayette Park, then up Connecticut Avenue, in unusually good cheer. It was one thing, as he'd often done in his career, to persuade an officer to buy a client's weapon system over some competitor's. It was another thing entirely—a level of influence that he'd never been interested in seeking—to help persuade the president of the United States to make any kind of momentous decision, much less to call off a war. Willoughby had concluded long ago that rational analysis and debate had no real impact on political decisions. This was the lesson that sparked his moment of disillusionment, the genesis of his subsequent career, the premise of a thousand decisions that molded the contours of his entire adult life. Was what he'd just witnessed an exception to this lesson? Or had he been wrong all these years? He found the latter possibility disturbing but also oddly exhilarating. A gush of self-satisfaction washed over him with such warm intensity, he almost forgot that he'd started the war in the first place.

Back in his office, he called to his aides. "Gupta! Manny Slaughter!" They came out into the foyer. "You did heroic work today. It's a rare moment in the lives of our ilk for a spree of archival research to sway the president of the United States and quite possibly alter the course of history. But we—the two of you and I—have done that today."

His assistants furtively glanced at each other, seemingly puzzled, even a little embarrassed, by the formality and emotion that had suddenly overtaken their normally insouciant boss.

"And Donna Cappella!" Willoughby exclaimed, turning to face her at her desk. "Your photographic prowess the other night would have made Weegee proud." He addressed his entire staff. "I'm giving you all a raise!"

He started toward his office, then turned back. "Actually, I may have to make that a one-time bonus. If I spend much more time saving the world, I won't make enough money to give you raises."

Willoughby entered his office, sat back in his chair, locked his hands behind his neck, and hoisted his feet up on his desk, extending his moment of glory. It was the first time he could remember in many years, maybe ever, when he felt true joy in that office without staring out the window or gazing at the jazz photographs on the wall. Could it be that he no longer needed the view of escape, or those images of another time and place, as a pathway to happiness? Could work alone—honest work—provide satisfaction enough?

The phone rang, interrupting his reverie. He sighed, straightened up, and answered it.

"Serge," said the caller in a slightly gravelly Russian accent. "This is Nikolai Rostov, your old dinner companion, you may recall."

"Yes, Nikolai," Willoughby replied wearily, hammered back down to earth.

"Tell me, Serge, what did your associates think of my proposal?"

"My *associates*?" Willoughby replied with a mix of amusement and frustration. "You mean my *contacts*?"

"Please, Serge, don't insult my intelligence," Rostov replied with a chuckle. "Just a little while ago, I was watching you on Fox News getting out of a limousine with the secretary of defense and walking alongside him into the West Wing of the White House for a very important meeting of the National Security Council."

Willoughby sighed. As often happened, a photo-op concocted for one set of viewers, in this case the Chinese, was interpreted in a less-than-welcome fashion by another set of viewers—the Russians. "In any event, I did pass on your message to my *contacts*. I haven't heard back from them."

"Now, listen, Serge," Rostov said, adopting a serious, even ominous tone. "If you and your *associates* are about to form an alliance with China, I must implore you, as I did during our dinner, that such an act is not in your country's interest. And I must *warn* you that it is not in *my* country's interest either. Our military exercises in the Black and Baltic Seas—which will get underway very soon—could be enlarged substantially, on little notice, and we can make trouble along the Chinese border near Vladivostok and in certain activities with our Syrian partners—"

"Nikolai, Nikolai," Willoughby interrupted. "I don't know where you're getting your information, but whatever might be going on between my country's government and China's, I seriously doubt there's the slightest suggestion of an *alliance*."

"I just hope that you keep in mind the totality of our dinner conversation when setting the agenda of any negotiations with Beijing," Rostov said in a very stilted tone.

"I will bring it up again with my associ—I mean, my *contacts*," Willoughby said, suddenly aware that this had been a very long day.

Rostov laughed, no doubt satisfied at having caught Willoughby in what he took as a Freudian slip, and hung up.

Willoughby figured he should phone Bloom. Along with Portis, Vollmer, and a few other officials, she had stayed in the Situation Room for a smaller meeting with the president after he and the underlings left, but it should have ended by now.

Bloom answered his call at once, and Willoughby told her about Rostov's phone call. "I don't know if his belligerence reflects Kremlin policy, but I thought you should know about it," he added.

Bloom sighed. "The fucking Russians. We're probably going to *have* to bring them in, but I'm glad you put him off this idea of an *alliance*, either with them or with the Chinese." She was speaking in a businesslike tone, as if she *were* talking with an associate, which Willoughby found slightly disorienting.

"So how did the meeting wind up?" he asked, exploiting their moment of collegiality.

"This is very confidential, but, as you probably surmised, the president is taking up the Chinese offer of a ceasefire. He is not accepting, at least not right now, any of their proposals for subsequent moves—the withdrawals to international waters, reimbursements for damage, and so forth. Nor is he open to conducting *formal* negotiations, not even a one-on-one with the Chinese president. But he's fine with having these issues discussed in upcoming *informal* talks."

"So," Willoughby replied, with some relief, "I guess the Mandelbaums will be working the back channel again. You won't need me to keep up this pretense any longer."

"I wish it were so, I *really* do," Bloom replied, "but I'm afraid we still need you. It turns out, during his lock-up and interrogation, Wolf suffered some heart palpitations and had to be rushed to the hospital. Nothing too serious, but he's not up to the task. And Chae-won is so pissed off that nobody from our side came to their rescue, she's washing her hands of the whole enterprise—not that I blame her."

She paused and took in a breath. "There's one more thing. The president was so impressed by the wonderful stunt that you and Portis pulled with the Cuban Missile Crisis tapes, he's decided to emulate Kennedy in every aspect—including keeping any deal, even any talks, with the Chinese a secret, just as JFK did with the Soviets. At least for now, he doesn't want any *officials* to meet with the Chinese, so that he can disavow direct involvement if the ceasefire collapses. The Chinese have no problem with that, and they still don't quite trust any of us, so, in their minds, you are still the man to deal with."

Willoughby sighed. "Look, Danica, I don't mind telling you, this has all been interesting and fun, but negotiating peace terms with the People's Republic of China drifts a bit outside my lane."

"No shit," Bloom replied dryly. "We'll figure out a way to hold your hand. Back to you soon."

Willoughby resumed his earlier pose, sitting back in his chair, propping his feet up on his deck. "Gupta! Get in here!" he called out.

Gupta appeared in Willoughby's doorway within seconds.

"What's the latest news?"

Gupta opened his notepad and rattled off his summary. "Fighting has dwindled considerably in the South China Sea, the Taiwan Strait, and up near North Korea. A few skirmishes with speedboats and flyovers, but nothing more. However, the Russians are making trouble. They've enlarged the mobilization for their upcoming military exercises in the Black Sea. And they're making some movements—vague but menacing—along the Russia-China border near Vladivostok."

Willoughby rolled his eyes. The Russians were actually doing what Rostov had warned him they *might* do. Clearly they were trying to disrupt what they saw as a possible US-China alliance, and they were speeding up their maneuvers—more quickly than even Rostov may have been notified—now that they knew (somehow they seemed to know) the American president was backing away from war. Bloom must have been referring to these troop movements when she said the Russians would probably have to be brought in on the talks.

"Finally," Gupta said, flipping the page in his notepad, "according to Natalie Gold in *The Gold Mine*, the president has fired General Vollmer as chairman of the Joint Chiefs of Staff."

Willoughby sat up straight. He went to Gold's website, typed in his passcode (which he'd been sharing with Gupta, so he too could keep up with her dispatches), and read her banner headline:

"VOLLMER FIRED OVER CHINA WAR."

He skimmed the first few paragraphs, then came to the key passage:

> One senior official told *The Gold Mine* that, in recent days, as conflict with China intensified, the president and Secretary of Defense Portis have both lost trust in Gen. Vollmer.
>
> According to several officials, Vollmer lied to Portis about the capabilities of a new, ultra-secret satellite system, which he claimed—apparently without foundation—could decisively strengthen the US position in an all-out war with the People's Republic of China.
>
> At an NSC Principals' Committee meeting today, the general lied to the entire Cabinet about the history of the 1962 Cuban Missile Crisis, claiming that President John F. Kennedy rejected a Soviet peace proposal to end the crisis—implying that the current Chinese peace proposal should be rejected as well.
>
> During the meeting, Portis played a declassified audiotape (Kennedy had secretly taped many of his meetings, including that one), proving that, in fact, Kennedy accepted the Soviet offer.

> The president fired Vollmer shortly after the NSC
> meeting in a smaller session, according to two inside
> sources.

"Jesus, she's fast," Willoughby said out loud. That meeting couldn't have broken up more than a half hour ago. He was so impressed with the speed of Gold's reporting and the depth of her sources that he momentarily forgot the main reason that he'd sat up to read her story: during the phone conversation just a few minutes earlier, Bloom had not mentioned Vollmer's ouster.

He was about to call her back, when he got another call, this one from Chas Greenway.

"Hey, Serge, I happen to be in your neck of the woods, thought I'd drop by, do you have a few minutes?" Greenway spoke in a hyper-casual, almost singsong tone, suggesting, if past was precedent, that in fact he had something very serious to say.

"Sure," Willoughby said, adopting a similar nonchalance. "Come on up."

"Um," Greenway replied, "let's meet at the park bench on the west side of the Circle instead."

After hanging up, Willoughby walked toward the door and started to tell Donna Cappella that he needed some air, but then had a thought: what if his much-too-careless friend had been followed? Was that why he didn't want to come up to the office? Recalling his dinner with Rostov and the photos taken by his versatile secretary, he turned her way with a smile. "Donna Cappella. Keen for another adventure?"

She looked up from the three computer screens that she'd been scanning in the course of accomplishing some complicated bookkeeping feat.

"You remember my friend Chas Greenway? He's been to the office a few times?"

"Oh, you mean the spy who came in with a hangover?" she asked drily.

Willoughby gulped. Was Chas drunk when he visited those times? Was his condition so obvious and persistent that Willoughby had stopped noticing? And how did she know that he worked for an intelligence agency? He vaguely remembered Greenway chatting her up, to no effect, one time when he dropped by. Did he tell her that he was a spy, in what would have been a comically futile attempt to impress her?

"Anyway," he replied, evading her question, "he's waiting for me on a park bench on the west side of Dupont Circle. Could you go ahead of me, sit a bit to the south, and see if there's anyone who seems to be watching us? If there is, don't take a picture this time. Just sort of point him out when I look over at you."

Donna Cappella saluted with excessive formality, stood up, and walked out the door. Willoughby waited a few minutes, then took the stroll to their meeting place. When he arrived, Greenway was already there, and Donna Cappella had assumed her lookout post.

"What's going on with you?" Greenway asked. "I saw you on TV walking with Portis into the White House. Are you working for the administration?"

"No," Willoughby waved the notion away. "Long, crazy story. I'll tell you sometime."

"Well, anyway, I have something that you need to see." Greenway took a folded piece of paper out of his jacket pocket. "Remember I told you that we've managed to turn a couple of the Chinese spies who'd been calling in coded messages to the Maryland hardware store? Well, they—and presumably all the spies that we haven't turned—got this query earlier today from their masters in Beijing."

He handed Willoughby the sheet of paper. Willoughby scanned it with alarm. It read:

What do you know about Serge Willoughby? Is he a trusted figure within the USA administration? Do his words and actions reflect official policy and genuinely peaceful intentions?

Willoughby took out his cell phone and called Bloom, who picked up on the first ring. "I need to come see you right away," he said.

"Serge, I was going to tell you about Vollmer's firing, but I had to wait until—"

"This is about something else," he interrupted. "Where are you?"

She was at the CIA's downtown offices, near the White House. She gave him the address and said one of her security people would meet him at the front door. "His name is Joseph. You'll recognize each other."

Willoughby was about to get up but first looked over at Donna Cappella. She nodded and motioned her head in a 45° angle toward the center of the circle. There, leaning against the bench near the fountain, was a man wearing sunglasses and a black suit, holding a camera. The second Willoughby spotted him, he turned away and took a picture of something that didn't seem particularly worth photographing.

"Let's go," Willoughby said to Greenway in an urgent tone.

They walked to the southern edge of the Circle and hailed a cab. As they got in, Willoughby noticed the man with the camera coming their way. He told the driver where to go, and as the taxi started down Connecticut Avenue, he saw his pursuer get in a cab right behind them.

"Turn right at the next intersection," Willoughby told the driver in a voice that was cooler and more collected than it would have been if he'd pulled this maneuver a week earlier.

"What are you doing?" Greenway asked. "He shouldn't be turning for another three blocks."

"We're being followed," Willoughby said quietly.

"What?" Greenway said skeptically, turning around for a look. "You're crazy."

The taxi turned right and drove halfway down the block.

"Now make a U-turn!" Willoughby told the driver, this time a bit more excited.

"I can't do that, it's illegal," the driver replied.

"Just do it! I'll pay if you get a ticket!" Willoughby responded.

The driver made a sharp U-turn, nearly hitting an oncoming car in the next lane. Before Willoughby could tell him to make a right, back onto Connecticut Avenue, a police siren screamed from behind them.

The driver moaned and pulled over. Greenway started laughing hysterically. The police officer poked his head in the cab's front window and asked for the driver's license and registration.

"*He* told me to do it!" the driver yelled, pointing to Willoughby in the back seat.

"Is that true?" the cop asked Willoughby in a Virginia drawl. "Why'd you do that?"

"I'm sorry, officer, it's a matter of national security," Willoughby replied, stumbling over his words.

Greenway laughed harder.

"I've heard a lot of stupid things blamed on *national security*," the cop said, "but an illegal U-turn takes the cake."

"Give *him* the ticket!" the driver screamed.

"Why should I give *him* the ticket?" the cop replied calmly. "*You're* driving the car. Would you crash through the White House gates if this guy told you to?" He looked at the two passengers. "Get *outta* here!" he told them, dripping with contempt.

Willoughby took out his wallet, gave the driver almost all of the bills, probably a hundred dollars or so, saving only a twenty and a one for himself, mumbling apologies to the driver and the cop while doing so, Greenway laughing harder still.

The two got out of the back seat and walked the rest of the way to the CIA's office.

"Look," Greenway said, gaining control of himself. "I know you've become a character in a true-life spy story, but that doesn't mean anyone's going to start following you."

"Donna Cappella pointed to someone back in the Circle who seemed to be looking at us a bit too closely," Willoughby explained.

"Oh, so now she's Mata Hari?" Greenway, the real spy, asked, and he laughed some more. "Listen, I saw that guy and the taxi he got into. Dark suit, sunglasses, camera, right? His cab drove off in the opposite direction. Nobody was following us."

They walked another block in silence, Willoughby a bit embarrassed, Greenway remaining silent, as if to avoid making his friend feel worse still. Finally, they arrived at Bloom's office building, one of the capital's ghastly new glass boxes. Joseph was standing outside the entrance. He was the same stocky figure with the comb-over that Willoughby had seen at the Chinese café in suburban Virginia and in the photographs from the rooftop restaurant where he dined out with Nikolai Rostov. Willoughby proceeded to the door. Joseph raised his hand to block Greenway from following. Greenway flashed a card, presumably his NSA ID pass. Joseph lowered his hand. All three went in and headed to an elevator.

The doors opened on the top floor. Joseph walked them to an office, where Bloom was sitting at a desk. She rose when they entered. It was a small, nondescript space—by design, Willoughby figured, reasoning that a hostile intruder would probably walk by, figuring it couldn't belong to the powerful director of the CIA.

"This is my contact at the other three-letter agency," Willoughby said by way of introducing Greenway. He then handed her the note from the Beijing spymasters and repeated what Greenway had said about its meaning and significance.

"Shit," Bloom said after reading it. "OK, I have to tell you something, and it is not to go outside this room." She waited for them to nod.

They did.

"We *just* learned that yesterday, General Vollmer phoned the Chinese army chief of staff to warn him that the White House would soon be making a peace proposal, that it's a phony offer, and that the person delivering it—and here he mentioned your name, *Serge Willoughby*—is not to be trusted. This note suggests the Chinese are canvassing their sources to see if you *are* to be trusted."

Willoughby sighed. "Well, Vollmer doesn't like me, I know that, but this is weird. Does he want war so much that he'd try to sabotage a peace deal put forth by the president of the United States? And why would the Chinese general believe him? Now that he's been fired, doesn't that discredit everything he's said?"

"Maybe," Bloom replied. "Trying to sabotage a peace deal is one reason why the president fired him. But the Chinese are at the very least confused, and Vollmer's warning might be enough to rile their own anti-peace faction."

Bloom paused for a few seconds, and Willoughby could practically see the wheels churning in her brain. He'd always found this trait, her palpable quantum-speed cogitation, one of the most appealing things about her.

"OK, we've got to do two things," she said, as if she'd just untangled all the complications. "First, Dr. Greenway—that's your name, right?"

"Yes," he replied warily, glancing at Willoughby, as if to ask, *"Did you tell her my name?"*

Willoughby shook his head and shrugged slightly.

"Who are the two Chinese spies that you've turned?" she asked. "I don't need to know their names. I mean, where do they work? Are they in a position to *know* whether or not Serge is a figure of any importance?"

"One of them is an upper-midlevel official in the Commerce Department," Greenway replied. "The other is a Washington businessman who does a lot of work with import-export permits all over Asia."

"So, they wouldn't know much, but they might know something," Bloom reflected. "Are these people *definitely* turned? Is it possible that they're triple agents? If you gave them a message to send to Beijing, would they do it without revealing that an American official had *told* them to send it?"

"We've given them messages to send back before, and they've gone through," Greenway replied. "We monitor all their communications. They're good."

"One more question," Bloom said. "Do you, as an NSA employee, mind doing something for me, the director of the CIA?"

Greenway shrugged and smiled. "I've committed so many acts of insubordination this week, I really don't care at this point."

Bloom laughed politely. "OK. Tell the spy at Commerce to write back something like this: 'I don't know Serge Willoughby personally, but based on what I've read and heard from senior officials in a position to know, he seems to be plugged in all over the national security bureaucracy, he's trusted as an intermediary among various agencies, and he's been a particularly active member of the peace faction when it comes to US-China relations.' Put it in your own words or his words, obviously. Once you've written it, send me a copy."

Greenway nodded. She shook his hand. "Thanks very much for doing this. Let me know if I can do anything for you. I have a feeling you'll want to ask for a favor sometime soon, so don't hesitate. Meanwhile, Joseph will call a car to take you anywhere."

Greenway took this as his cue to leave.

"Now," Bloom said, shifting tones and turning to Willoughby. "You and I have to be seen together at that little Chinese café out in Virginia. We have to go there right now. I assume you have nothing better to do."

For nearly the entire forty-five-minute car ride from downtown Washington to the strange Chinese diner, Bloom, sitting in the backseat next to Willoughby, feverishly tapped the keys of her phone, presumably texting or emailing several colleagues. She was interrupted twice by voice calls, each of which lasted only a few seconds. Her side of the conversations, which was all Willoughby could hear, went like this: "Yes... No... Do it... Now," and "No fucking way... Call him... Ten minutes ago."

Willoughby tapped away on his phone too, in part to keep up appearances, though also to look up news sites. The *Times* was reporting that Vollmer had been responsible for the arrest of Wolf Mandelbaum. Willoughby knew this was untrue, but it struck him as a clever cover story. He was also impressed that this detail was not in Natalie Gold's dispatch, suggesting that, even though her reporting had an agenda ("to save the world"), she wouldn't sink to publishing a phony cover story for that purpose.

A half hour into the ride, Bloom put down her phone and turned to Willoughby. "OK, here's what's about to happen. The manager of the Chinese café where we're going is a second cousin of our main source in the Chinese back channel. You and I are going to eat dinner there now, so that he can see us together. He'll tell his second cousin you're with me, and that will shore up your credibility. Between this and the note that your friend Greenway sends back to Beijing, any damage done by Vollmer should be repaired."

"So, what happens after this?" Willoughby asked.

"What happens after this is the big meeting," Bloom replied. "That's what I've been texting like mad about, and that's the other thing you and I need to discuss. As you can imagine, the China hands in the NSC and the State Department aren't pleased that you're the one who's going to these talks. They all know who you are, they've all recently read the China war study you did for the Marines, and they're impressed by it. But they also know that you know next to nothing about Chinese politics or foreign policy."

"May I remind you," Willoughby interjected, "that I did not volunteer for this role?"

"And may I remind *you*," Bloom shot back, "that you're the one who started this war? So don't fuck this up, Serge. Don't pull a Jimmy Carter."

"What's Jimmy Carter got to do with this?"

"Oh." Bloom sighed. "Long story, short version. Back in 1994, we were close to war with North Korea—I mean, *very* close, much closer than most outsiders knew. Ex-President Carter offered to go to North Korea and calm things down—Kim Il-sung had been inviting him to come visit ever since he got voted out of the White House—and President Clinton let him go, but under *strict* instructions not to negotiate any deals while he was over there. Well, Carter spends three days on Kim's yacht. Next thing you know, he calls the White House, giving them five minutes' notice that he's about to go live on CNN, where he'll outline the terms of a treaty that he and Kim worked out, shutting down North Korea's plutonium processing plant in exchange for massive economic aid from the US."

"I remember that," Willoughby said. "The treaty that grew out of their deal was pretty successful, right? It kept North Korea from building atom bombs for about eight years, if I recall."

"Yes," Bloom snapped, a bit impatient, "but China isn't North Korea, you're not meeting with the leader of any country, and, above all, you're not Jimmy Carter. The point is, don't go rogue, Serge."

By this time, Bloom's driver was pulling into the café parking lot. When the car stopped, someone opened the back door. It was Joseph, her security guard. He'd been sitting in the front seat, riding shotgun, this whole time. Willoughby then noticed a car pulling up behind them. Two more security men, who'd been trailing her car got out and approached Joseph.

The five of them—Willoughby, Bloom, Joseph, and the other two, whose names he wasn't told—entered the restaurant. The café was three-quarters full, and everyone looked up when they walked through the door. They made quite the impression, and that was the intent: Bloom, so authoritative in her black business suit, low-cut white blouse, and shining turquoise broach; the security guards, all brawny, no-nonsense; and Willoughby, nondescript but drenched in prestige through his association with the others.

Willoughby and Bloom sat down at a corner table while the security team staked out separate positions between the table and the door.

"The dinner food is slightly better than the breakfast," Bloom said unenthusiastically.

A waiter came by immediately to take their order. Without looking at a menu, which hadn't been offered in any case, Bloom asked for several dishes, none of them familiar to Willoughby, who at this point was going along for the ride in every sense of the phrase. The waiter walked away with the order.

Bloom tilted her head toward a Chinese man in a white jacket behind the nearby bar. "See that guy on the phone, standing at attention? That's the manager. Judging from his erect posture, he's probably talking to his second cousin. Your street cred is riding high."

From the time they walked to their table, Willoughby had noticed the man in question looking, almost gawking, at him, as if Willoughby were some sort of celebrity. He tried to stay cool.

Bloom explained that she'd had the café scanned on several occasions and knew it wasn't bugged, but still, she didn't want to be overheard by the surrounding diners, most of whom were probably spies of one sort or another. This was why she sat with her back facing the rest of the room, so no one could read her lips.

"So, here's the thing about this upcoming meeting," she continued, stern and businesslike but quiet. "Both presidents, ours and China's, are very nervous about *any* sort of meeting. Tensions between our countries have been so fraught, even before the fighting broke out, we haven't held serious talks about anything for ages. Certainly we can't hold official talks while there's still bloodshed. That's why no officials will be at this upcoming meeting. In fact, if a spokesman is asked, the meeting isn't happening. If a spokesman is asked in the future, the meeting never took place, or if it did take place, it was some informal, exploratory conclave set up by a few people who play no role in either government. That way, if it all goes south, there will be no record that anything resembling peace talks ever took place. Better not to have tried than to try and fail."

"Who is going to be there?" Willoughby asked.

"It's going to be you, your Pentagon consultant pal Isaiah Douglass, and your dinner buddy Nikolai Rostov, which we don't much like, but now that the Russians have shoved their way into this confrontation, it's probably best that they take part. I'm also sending one of my special assistants, John Smith, who will do the technical set-up, as well as some security people, who will hang around the periphery. We're going to be listening in remotely—me, the president, Secretary Portis, a few other senior officials—and we'll run the audio through our hot lines to Moscow and Beijing, in real time, so they can listen too. "

She paused and arched her eyebrows. He nodded, as if to say, *Yes, I understand that this is a very big deal.*

"Now there's been a bit of a twist on the Chinese side," she went on. "Their delegate is not going to be our source in the usual back channel. That guy's a diplomat at the UN, and, as I said, there can't be any official connection. So, they're flying over a major figure from Beijing. His name is Wu Chao-xiang. He's the intermediary between the back channel and the Chinese Communist Party's Central Committee. He has advanced degrees in economics and physics. He's also a huge oligarch. He essentially runs China's military-industrial complex. And he's related somehow to the president. In other words, he's a big, big deal. "

Willoughby didn't know whether to feel important or in way over his head.

"But here's the important thing, Serge," Bloom said, raising her voice, despite her efforts at discretion. "This is not going to be a *negotiating* session. You are *not* going to walk out of the meeting with a peace accord or *any* sort of accord—hence my reference to Jimmy Carter. The whole idea, and the only idea, is to make sure that all parties are agreed, first, to ending hostilities for a fairly long period of time and, second, to starting negotiations in the very near future on how to keep the peace. And that's *all*. Our guidance is that you should speak as little as possible."

"That's fine with me," Willoughby said. "When is this happening?"

"Soon, maybe tomorrow," Bloom replied, suddenly looking a little nervous.

"And *where?*"

"We don't know yet. It has to be in New York because that's where Wu wants to go, nonnegotiable. We can't have it at any of our UN missions, it can't be in any government facility, because—again—this can't look as if it has an official imprimatur."

Willoughby smiled and his eyes widened. "I know the perfect place."

CHAPTER 11

The Comedy Cellar was one of Willoughby's half dozen favorite spots in New York City, and the only one in a neighborhood—the heart of Greenwich Village—that, structurally, had barely changed not just in his lifetime but over the previous century. To the west sprawled Sixth Avenue (its formal name, Avenue of the Americas, had never caught on), its wide lanes of dense traffic careening toward glass towers jutting in distant Midtown. To the east lay the expanding corporate empire of New York University. But in between, on MacDougal Street, a crumbly, narrow road, on the block between West Third and Bleecker Streets, stood a row of time-stands-still brick buildings erected in the nineteenth century—originally artisan factories, now restaurants, bars, bodegas, nightclubs, an ice cream parlor, a record shop, a tattoo joint—none more than five stories high, some with their arched windows and cornices still extant. In the '60s, before Willoughby's time, this block of MacDougal was a Mecca for beatniks and hippies. The Gaslight, a folk-music-and-poetry coffeehouse where Kerouac, Ginsberg, and Dylan hung out, was just across the street. The San Remo Club, where the Gaslight crowd went for harder drinks, was just down the block. Only a few figments from that era survived—Caffe Reggio (the alleged site of America's first cappuccino), Minetta Tavern, and Café Wha'—but the sidewalks still teemed with life into the wee hours.

Willoughby had discovered the Comedy Cellar more than ten years earlier, by accident, during one of his solo weekend jaunts to Manhattan. He had been strolling along MacDougal, gazing at the sites of rebel American culture, imagining the vibe of the street back in its heyday, when he came upon the Cellar's marquee, blazing in neon bulbs. This was before the renaissance in stand-up comedy; anyone could walk in off the street and get a seat, and that's what Willoughby did. At college, during his phase of exploring everything he'd never seen, heard or tasted on the commune, he collected record albums of the earlier era's edgier comedians—Lenny Bruce, Mort Sahl, Jonathan Winters, Nichols & May—but he'd never seen a stand-up show in person. The set at the Cellar that night rekindled and deepened his enthusiasm for the artform. He suddenly recognized stand-up comedy, in its highest form, as a sort of science, a verbal ballet of precision rhythm. A micro-beat shift in timing, or a half-decibel accent of emphasis, could mean the difference between a laugh and cricket silence, between killing an audience and bombing. The acts—the good ones—seemed completely spontaneous, but they'd been thoroughly developed, endlessly practiced, meticulously refined.

Willoughby now reflected that the same could be said of his other extracurricular passions: jazz, basketball, urban street photography. They were a relief from his daily drudgery, but, as he now realized, they weren't as huge a departure from his professional life as he'd figured. They all reflected, and validated, his core sensibility—a predilection for mathematical exactitude—and (here was the key thing) combined it with aesthetic pleasure: with art, wit, and beauty.

Musing on this connection , he wondered if picking the Cellar as the place for the big meeting was, perhaps subconsciously, a way for him to fuse his personal and professional lives, to take his stovepiped passions—which he'd deliberately kept separate, to avoid the mind-trashing trap of chasing Grand Universal Theories—and snap them into singularity: a life more coherent, infused with both pleasure and... there it was, the word that Natalie Gold threw at him... *purpose.*

After the comedy set on that first, revelatory night long ago, Willoughby had wandered upstairs to the Olive Tree, the café just above the Cellar, and soon found himself in conversation with the owner of both establishments, an amiably argumentative musician and ex-lawyer named Noam Dworman. On his next few trips to New York, Willoughby made a point of going back to the Cellar— sometimes after a jazz set at the Village Vanguard, just a ten-minute walk away—and then noshing at the Olive Tree, where he and Dworman, who were roughly the same age, would talk about music, comedy, politics, and the travails of operating a small business.

When Willoughby told Danica Bloom that the Comedy Cellar would be a perfect place for the secret meeting with the Chinese and the Russians, her jaw dropped and her eyes widened.

"The *Cellar?*" she practically shouted. "You've got to be shitting me." The two of them had once gone to the Cellar, back when they were a couple. It might have been their final date. If he recalled correctly, she didn't laugh much.

"Not *in* the Cellar, but upstairs," Willoughby clarified.

The Cellar, he reminded her, was on the ground floor, or actually, as the name suggested, a few steps below ground level. The Olive Tree took up the second floor. Two stories above that, through an entrance invisible from the street, was an apartment, where Dworman's stepmother, an artist only a few years older than Noam, lived and worked. (Dworman's father, who had died many years earlier, started the Cellar in the early '80s; this was his second, much younger wife.)

If Willoughby could swing it with Dworman and his stepmother, the meeting could take place in the apartment. It was suitably spacious and quiet: the front half, the living area, was closed off from the din of MacDougal Street by double-paned glass and dark shades; the back half, the art studio, looked out on the calm of Minetta Lane, a curved, narrow back alley unlike any other street in Manhattan, more like a Parisian ruélle.

Bloom was skeptical, but having no good alternatives and facing a tight deadline, she told Willoughby to go ahead and ask if the space was available. He sent Dworman a text, appealing to his interest in world news and history:

> Noam—I'm coming to NYC soon, maybe tomorrow. Could you let me use the apartment for a Top Secret diplomatic meeting that might end the war with China? I'm serious. I'm serious about the "Top Secret" part, too. Don't tell anybody that I'm even asking…
> Serge

Less than two minutes later, Dworman wrote back:

> Serge, Of course! Very excited. Will tell nobody (loose lips sink ships). No problems with the

apartment. Stepmom is in New Orleans for a week, visiting friends, but even if she were here, I'd tell her to get lost. Noam

"It's on," Willoughby told Bloom.

"OK," she replied with a sigh. "While you were texting your pal, I was texting my people. If all goes well, the meeting will happen tomorrow at four PM. Someone will pick you up outside your apartment around eleven AM and drive you to Andrews, where you and the others will take an Agency plane to JFK."

She reached into her briefcase, pulled out a two-inch-thick binder, and handed it to him. "Here's some background material. Read all of it before you leave for the airport."

Back in his apartment, Willoughby stayed up late, sitting in his favorite Art Deco chair, browsing the materials that Bloom had given him—a mix of issue briefs, FAQs, and biographical portraits—while nursing a snifter of brandy. Wafting at low volume from his stereo was the Kronos Quartet's CD of Phillip Glass string compositions, which Willoughby sometimes played to focus his mind and soothe his anxieties—not many albums could do both.

At one point, during a break, he looked around at the cozy cocoon he'd fashioned for himself over the previous few decades. The plush carpets, mainly Kilims and Cimaks that he'd purchased on a onetime trip to Turkey. The oak bookshelves crammed with a thousand or more volumes, many of them treasures scraped from endless hours of leisurely hunts through second-hand book shops. The art, including the Feinstein photos, a Rauschenberg etching, an array of first-edition movie posters, and a Motherwell collage that he'd bought for a song at an estate auction attracting bidders for antique furniture who apparently knew nothing about art. Off to the side, the stereo system, pieced together from different brands of components after several months of careful listening at audio salons, a process that befuddled most of his friends—Chas Greenway, whom he brought along to one hi-fi trade fair, thought the whole enterprise was madness—though the resulting sound, when spinning a well-engineered recording, could transport him to another time and place, which was where he wanted to be through most of his life, escape being the main point of his most passionate pursuits.

He had no regrets about any of this, but, as he sat reading his issues briefs, the result of having plunged himself and the world into a serious crisis, he now wondered whether he might have burrowed into his well-crafted pleasure-cave, eluding the world's more challenging complications, all too thoroughly.

At around midnight, the phone rang.

"Serge, it's Natalie." The voice was insistent but welcome.

"Long time, no hear," Willoughby said as casually as he could manage. "You've been doing ace work."

"What's this I hear about you going to New York tomorrow to talk peace with the Chinese and Russians?" she asked in a way that sounded more like an accusation than a question.

"I don't know if I should be talking to you about this," Willoughby replied coyly.

"Come on, Serge, I know everything, you know that," she said, a bit coquettish but serious enough that Willoughby couldn't comfortably dodge her inquisitiveness. "Exactly where is this meeting happening?"

"You know it's in New York, but you don't know exactly where?" he replied, trying to be playful. "I'm disappointed."

"I could have found out by making two phone calls, but I thought I'd call *you*," she said, hitting the ball back in his court, pushing all of his buttons.

Willoughby hesitated. "I'm assuming this is an authorized call," he said, figuring that she and Bloom stayed in frequent contact with each other. "Do you know the Comedy Cellar?"

"Sure, I went there all the time when I studied at Barnard. The meeting is at the *Cellar?*"

"It's in the top-floor apartment," he said, musing on the pleasing coincidence that Gold liked stand-up comedy. "The meeting is supposed to start around four o'clock. I don't think even Danica would let you ride with me on the CIA's plane. So go to New York, get to the club when you can, hang out at the Olive Tree, and I'll look for you when it's over."

Willoughby got a call the next morning at 8:00 saying the car would pick him up an hour earlier than scheduled, because of heavy traffic on the roads leading out of Washington. A black sedan picked him up at precisely 10:00. The driver nodded and grunted as he got in the back seat.

As he'd been warned, the moment they hit I-295, the lanes jammed with cars, vans, and buses, and movement slowed to a crawl.

"What's going on with the traffic?" Willoughby asked.

"Evacuation," the driver replied laconically.

"Evacuation?" Willoughby asked.

"The war. People think it's going to go nuclear," the driver said with a sigh. "They're headed to the coast or up north."

Clearly, Willoughby mused, they hadn't heard about the ceasefire. He phoned Bloom. She answered on the first ring. "Hey, Danica, the traffic is crazy. The driver says people are evacuating. Is something going on that I don't know about?"

Bloom paused. "Not to worry. You'll get to Andrews on time."

"I don't doubt that," Willoughby clarified, "I'm just wondering if there's anything new about the war."

Bloom paused again. "Well, look, as the president made clear, the ceasefire is a private agreement, no one's announced it, so we're all still poised to resume fighting. The warships are within a short-range missile shot from one another, fighter-bombers are circling overhead. If the meeting goes south, we all go back to where we were. You didn't understand this?"

"No, not really. I thought the meeting was going to be pro forma, and I'm supposed to keep my mouth shut."

"Well, I didn't want to make you nervous," Bloom said in an unconvincing stab at reassurance. "Don't worry, you'll do fine." She hung up.

Finally, after a nearly two-hour drive, an hour longer than usual but exactly as anticipated on this morning, they pulled into the gates of Andrews Air Force Base. A husky, suited man—he wasn't Joseph, Bloom's main security guard, but he might have frequented the same gym and tailor—met the sedan near the runway and escorted Willoughby to the small plane.

Three other security guards, similar in appearance, were already onboard, as were Ike Douglass and Bloom's special assistant, John Smith.

Willoughby sat next to Douglass.

"Danica just told me that the war isn't at all over."

Douglass shrugged. "You thought it was?" He chuckled. "Too late to worry now. Did you read the briefing book?"

"Yeah. The Chinese guy has a pretty stunning résumé. I wonder what *their* briefing book says about *me*. If I come off as impressive as he does, then I'm guessing *our* books are bullshit, too."

"Grade inflation all around." Douglass snorted. "So the bosses can pretend that the world is in good hands."

Willoughby looked around the cabin, an eight-passenger Gulfstream jet, not the most luxurious model but comfortable enough. He took a closer look at John Smith, who sat on the opposite side of the plane, silently entombed in dark sunglasses and ear buds. "What's with this John Smith?"

"I don't know," Douglass replied. "The one time that I met him before, his name was Jim Jones." He laughed. "CIA has a lot of people like that."

Less than a minute later, the plane took off and Douglass promptly fell asleep. Willoughby supposed that people who traveled a lot—and Douglass traveled frequently with Portis—had a knack for catching some shut-eye at a moment's notice.

Inspired by the thought, Willoughby took out his own custom earbuds, plugged them into his phone, clicked on the Qobuz music-server app, and called up "Stolen Moments" from Oliver Nelson's *The Blues and the Abstract Truth*, one of the coolest jazz tunes and a perfect mood-setting prelude for an absurdly unlikely meeting where

Willoughby would need to contrive and display a façade of unflappable confidence.

It was a warm, breezy day in New York City. Willoughby rolled down the window as the van sped down the FDR Drive: to his left, the East River, glistening with the sunlight's reflections; to his right, Manhattan's syncopated skyline, clean, sharp, and inviting, against a cloudless blue sky. The driver turned off at the Houston Street exit, and so did the Gershwin-hummed reverie, as the swift cruise along the expressway shifted to a concrete quagmire of clogged traffic and snarling horns. It took almost as long to slog through the two miles from the Houston Street exit to the Comedy Cellar as it had taken to traverse the twenty-two miles from JFK to the exit. Willoughby knew this was why some people didn't much like New York—too crowded, too noisy—but he took pleasure even from the city's grittier aspects, at least in the small doses an occasional visit supplied.

His only fellow passenger was Douglass, who took the long ride as an opportunity for another snooze. John Smith and the security crew had taken a different car, which was last seen weaving in and out of the expressway's lanes with daredevil abandon.

By the time Willoughby and Douglass arrived at the Cellar, John Smith and the crew were already up in the apartment, checking for blind spots and setting up the communications gear. Chinese and Russian security agents were there too, and John Smith—who, up till this point, hadn't said a word, at least not in Willoughby's presence—was laughing it up with them, rapt in spirited conversation, seamlessly shifting from English to Russian to Mandarin and back again, as if they knew one another from some international spy convention. And maybe they did. The scene reminded Willoughby of a meeting he had with an officer in the Pentagon's public affairs department a few decades earlier, not long after the start of his career as a consultant. He'd asked the officer about a gold-plated trophy displayed prominently on his desk. The officer proudly replied that it was the top prize in a recent international festival of recruitment and propaganda films produced by various defense ministries, including those of the Soviet Union and China. It struck Willoughby at the time as bizarre: this was near the height of Cold War tensions, yet the putative rivals in the twilight struggle were sharing—as if they were competitive colleagues in a common commercial industry—the cinematic ads they'd created to paint each another as mortal enemies worth killing in combat. Over time, Willoughby came to realize the contest and the trophy weren't so bizarre; the whole national security enterprise was theater, and John Smith's camaraderie with his Russian and Chinese counterparts reaffirmed that view.

So why, he wondered, *are we now all mired on the brink of a world war?*

A few minutes later, Nikolai Rostov arrived, smiling and chuckling as he approached Willoughby with his hand extended. "So, all this," Rostov said, waving his free hand at the agents, the communication gear, and the rest, "is the work of your *contacts*, is it?"

Willoughby shrugged and smirked. There was no denying it: he was, as Rostov had put it in their last phone conversation and again just now, an *associate*, at least for the next few hours

Finally, in walked Wu Chao-xiang, fresh from Beijing, elegantly coiffed, decked out in a dark blue pinstriped suit, white shirt, and red tie, much in the style of a Western diplomat or business executive, except for the yellow-starred red-flag brooch pinned to his lapel. He looked a lot like China's president—the same furrowed brow, slicked-down hair, and prominent cheekbones.

Things were running late. It was 5:30 by the time the technical gear was set up and the players all arrived. A table and four chairs had been arranged in the back room, the art studio, where the meeting was taking place. The stepmother's paintings were displayed, some hung up, some stacked against the walls. A few of them were watercolors of Greenwich Village tenements and townhouses; most were oil paintings, some on large canvasses, mainly portraits of women, several in various stages of undress.

Wu surveyed the room, scrutinizing the artworks. "Are these for sale?" Wu asked Willoughby, a good sign that he considered the least-qualified person in the room to be in charge.

"I don't know," Willoughby replied. "You can ask the artist's stepson after our meeting. He owns the café and comedy club downstairs."

"There's a comedy club downstairs?" Wu asked. He seemed intrigued.

Willoughby nodded.

John Smith interrupted the conversation. "Director Bloom needs to talk with you urgently," he quietly told Willoughby, handing him a phone and pointing to the door.

"Excuse me for a moment," Willoughby said with a nod to Wu and Rostov, and stepped out in the hallway. "Yes, Madame Director," he said, putting on a tone of formality in case anyone overheard him.

"Listen, Serge, we got hold of the intel report about you in the Chinese briefing book," Bloom said.

"Funny," he replied, "I was wondering what it might say."

"They're on to you," she said, a bit hurried in her speech. "They know all about your MO at Janus Corporation, how you come to one conclusion in a study for one client, then the opposite conclusion in a study for another client."

Willoughby gulped.

"But here's the thing," she went on. "They *like* it. They see it as a sign that you know the ins and outs of all the bureaucratic factions, and they see your profiting from it as—let me find the exact quote here… ah, here it is, '*quintessentially American.*' They see your recent activities—the briefing of Portis and the Joint Chiefs, your appearance at the NSC meeting, your dinner with Rostov, your breakfast and dinner with me—as a continuation of your games-playing, but for peaceful ends. And they see the president's firing of General Vollmer and approval of this meeting as a sign that your tactics are working. Their only uncertainty seems to be whether you've commandeered this shift in US policy or whether you're acting as the winning faction's chief agent. Either way, they see your word as *the* word. So, play on your instincts. Just don't fuck it up."

She hung up before Willoughby had a chance to ask if this still meant he should keep his mouth shut or if he should feel free to blather on and, if so, what he should blather on about.

He reentered the apartment, handed the phone back to John Smith, and nodded to Wu and Rostov. Wu snapped his fingers, and in one motion, the security teams from all three countries left the room, taking up positions either outside the door or downstairs on the sidewalk.

The four players—Willoughby, Douglass, Rostov, and Wu— took their seats around the table. John Smith, sitting a few feet away and now wearing a phone operator's headset, turned on the equipment. By prior agreement, the transmission was to be audio only. If an audiotape were leaked, it would be hard to prove whose voices could be heard; its authenticity, and certainly its importance, could easily be denied. Video, by contrast, would be all too revealing.

John Smith asked his superiors in Washington if they could hear him. They affirmed that they could. Their counterparts in Moscow and Beijing said the signal was coming through loud and clear on their ends too.

"I would like to begin," Wu declared. "First, I want to thank Dr. Willoughby and Colonel Douglass for organizing this meeting. Gospodin Rostov, I thank you as well for your attendance."

Rostov flashed Wu a nasty look.

"But I must preface our conversation with a statement of general concern. In all the decades of our existence, the People's Republic of China has never initiated armed conflict against a foreign state. We have certainly never occupied foreign territory—whereas, in this same time span, the USA has started countless wars and occupied, at times, whole nations and continents of foreign land."

He looked over at Willoughby, then at Douglass, with an impenetrable expression. "You have done this under the pretense, perhaps the delusional belief, of 'spreading democracy'"—here he held up and bent the first two fingers of both hands, signifying quotation marks—"or 'upholding international norms.' But America does not hold a monopoly on the concept of democracy. For proof, you can read any history on your Indian Wars, or the lynchings of Black people in the South, or the quite recent violence against your own citizens of Asian or Muslim birth. There is a Chinese concept of democracy, a Russian concept of democracy, all kinds of democracy, yet the People's Republic of China does not wage war—or support others waging wars—on behalf of its concept."

Willoughby felt dizzy. This was not at all how the meeting was supposed to go. *Did the Chinese set us up? Is Beijing preparing more strikes against American ships, planes, and satellites at this moment when our guard is down?* Were he, Douglass, and the others going to step out of the meeting—after however long it took Wu to wrap up his harangue—with the mission failed and the war resuming at full blast?

Wu paused briefly, ostensibly to take a sip of water but also to pull a sheet of paper out of a folder at his side. He showed it to the others around the table. It read, in all caps:

> DON'T WORRY. I HAVE TO TALK LIKE THIS
> RIGHT NOW. IT'S FOR POLITICS. IT IS NOT
> SERIOUS. I WILL GET DOWN TO BUSINESS
> IN A FEW MINUTES.

Once they read the message and sighed in relief, Wu flashed a smile and a wink, and proceeded with another five minutes of anti-imperialist bombast.

After he finished, Rostov, not to be outflanked, started up his own monologue: "The Russian Federation has played the role of peacekeeper and freedom-lover in countless conflicts around the world—conflicts in which either the USA or China, or both, exerted a nefarious influence." This went on for several minutes.

Willoughby sensed it was now his role in this charade to turn the narrative around, using Bloom's frantic message—*"They know who you are, so exploit it"*—as a guide. "Gentlemen, let us confront the fundamental issues," Willoughby began, not quite sure what those issues were or what he would say next. "Yes, the United States has its faults, but our people, even our leaders, acknowledge them, confront them, try to fix them. We also are a nation of free thinking and differences of opinion, a quality reflected in the division of powers within our government. As you know, I have spent much of my professional life straddling opposing factions, seeking common ground between them"—he could imagine Bloom and Portis rolling their eyes at this—"and, in the past few days of crisis, I have been involved in forming a coalition to dial back this war. We in this room have been sent here by our respective leaders, under the cloak of secrecy, to agree on a ceasefire and the beginnings of a peace of sorts, which will then be formally hammered out by our official negotiators. Can we agree on this?"

Wu clapped his hands. "Very good, Dr. Willoughby, a very laudable presentation. You too, Gospodin Rostov. So, our part of the show is over. We have indeed said the things that we were sent here to say. Now I am going to say a few more things."

He stood up and moved closer to John Smith's microphone set-up, so the officials back in all three capitals could hear him as clearly as possible. "I have studied the literature on war and peace and deterrence, and there is a paradox—potentially a tragic paradox—in its logic. The basic idea of deterrence—and let us begin with *nuclear* deterrence because all three of our countries are nuclear powers—is that each of us convinces the others that we really will drop the bomb in response to aggression. Part of this process involves convincing *ourselves* that we would actually use nuclear weapons. Convincing ourselves, as well as others, requires building certain types of missiles and devising certain war plans that would *enable* us to use nuclear weapons. And before you know it, a strategy to *deter* nuclear war becomes synonymous with a strategy to *fight* and, if possible, to *win* a nuclear war. If a crisis ever arose, this logic would encourage— would almost *require*—escalating the cycle of threats and counterthreats, to the point where deterrence and war converge, in order to maintain what we call *credibility*."

He paused for dramatic effect. "Would we ever actually use nuclear weapons? I don't know. But for deterrence to work, for it to remain *credible*, we have to *behave* as if we would—yet that increases the chance that we *actually* would."

He paused again. "This is where we are now. We are at the point in this war where we must continue to escalate—possibly all the way to nuclear war—or back off. We are treading on virgin ground. No nuclear power has ever deployed its armed forces to wage war against the armed forces of another nuclear power, and that is what we are now doing. Shall we proceed or back off? Considering the question so starkly, I would say there is no choice *but* to back off. Clausewitz wrote that war is politics by other means. What *politics*—what political objectives—could justify the horrors of nuclear war? And yet by backing off, we are encouraging others to think we might be *generally* unwilling to use nuclear weapons, not just in this crisis but ever. Does this encourage some aggressor to make a violent move, unafraid of the consequences?"

Willoughby and Douglass looked at each other and raised their eyebrows. This guy was more clever, and this crisis suddenly seemed to trigger more dangers, than Willoughby had figured.

"Now we cannot talk about this openly or perhaps not even in this closed conversation," Wu went on. "If any of us—especially if any of you, esteemed leaders—so much as raised the possibility, for a moment, that you might *not* go all the way to nuclear war in response to an armed attack that threatened your vital interests, well, then deterrence falls apart, and in some ways war, even a string of wars, becomes *more* likely in the future. I may be eroding deterrence and increasing the chance of war simply by saying these things. You may be complicit in my sin simply by *listening* to me and *acknowledging* that there is perhaps a bit of truth in what I say."

Wu paused and cleared his throat.

"So, *are* you listening? Are you acknowledging that we may be heightening the chance of war in the future, for the sake of backing away from the war we are fighting now?"

There was dead silence on the other end. Finally, Bloom spoke up. "I'm sorry," she said, a nervous hesitation in her voice. "I think we lost your connection for a couple minutes, Dr. Wu. The last thing we heard was you complimenting Dr. Willoughby for his laudable presentation."

The other listeners in the capitals concurred. "Yes." "Da, pravil'no." "En, nà jiù duìle."

"But we take your point," Bloom continued, "and you can rest assured—I think I'm speaking for everyone—that this meeting has had the desired effect. We will jointly and publicly declare a ceasefire tomorrow, then swiftly assemble a working group in Geneva to hammer out the details of a new status quo."

"Thank you very much, gentlemen," the president said. Then he hung up.

All four men on MacDougal Street sat silent for a few seconds, then roared with laughter. Even John Smith couldn't help smiling.

"Tell me, Mr. Smith," Willoughby asked. "Is it possible that they really did lose connection?"

For a few seconds, John Smith appeared to weigh loyalty to his bosses against pride in his technical prowess. The latter won out. "Absolutely no fucking way."

The foursome howled with laughter again, this time joined by John Smith. But Wu's monologue hit a chord with Willoughby. This meeting, the whole defense establishment, the entire system of international security—they all teetered on the deception of believing two contradictory things at once and hoping that nobody noticed. He now saw this truth more clearly than ever. The whole world, it seemed, was one big Janus Corporation.

As they packed up to leave the apartment, Willoughby approached Wu. "You seemed intrigued about the comedy club downstairs. The opening set starts in a few minutes. It will last about an hour and a quarter. There's an MC who warms up the crowd, gets them laughing, then introduces five or six stand-up comedians, one at a time. I've looked at the lineup. It's a very strong group of comedians. Do you want to go watch?" He addressed the rest of the group. "Should we all go down and watch the stand-up comedy show? It could be our celebration."

"Yes, let's do that," Wu said.

"Yes, it sounds like fun," Rostov added.

"I'd also like to ask the owner about buying one of these paintings," Wu added.

Surrounded by their security details, the four men went down two flights of stairs to the Olive Tree, which was still fairly empty. Noam Dworman, sitting at the bar, watched them come in.

Willoughby went over, smiled, and shook his hand. "It worked. We hammered out a peace. Now we all want to go see the show. There are five of us, and a few security guards will have to stand nearby."

"No, just four of us," Douglass said. "Mr. Smith had to leave in a hurry."

"Follow me." Dworman led the group down the backroom steps from the café to the Cellar, the private stairway that the comedians took when it was their turn to go on. Willoughby pointed toward an empty table—one of the few remaining—just to the right of the stage. Dworman asked a waitress to seat the group there.

Wu and Rostov looked around, as if they were in a strange and exotic land, which, in a way, they were. The Cellar was a small, dank room, wide but not very deep, with bare pipes strewn across the low ceiling. (The taller comedians could touch it with no great stretch.) At the front and center was a stage, though it was barely a stage, elevated just one step above the audience. Behind it was a brick wall, and about a foot in front of the wall was a stand with a microphone waiting to be held. The club was packed, as was true of nearly every set, every night, and the preshow chatter reverberated off the walls, a seamless din of anticipatory revelry.

Just as the odd foursome took their seats, the house lights dimmed, a music track blared through the speakers, and a prerecorded announcer introduced the MC. The crowd applauded wildly.

The MC was one of the regulars, a tall Black man with a baritone voice and an easy smile. Willoughby had seen him a couple times before. He was very funny, very skilled at engaging the audience. "Welcome to the Comedy *Cellll-larrrr!*" he hollered, and the crowd cheered some more. He put on a mock-horrified expression. "What the fuck are you all doing here? Haven't you heard we're in a *war*? Shouldn't you all have hauled your asses to your country homes or your beach houses?" He laughed a little. "We're called the Comedy *Cellar*, but, as you may have noticed, we're just two inches underground. This isn't a fallout *shelter*. If they drop an atom bomb on New York City, you're all fried motherfuckers—nothing we can do about it."

The audience tittered nervously.

"Anyone here from another country?" It was a standard line that allowed comedians to tell jokes that they'd written, sometimes years earlier, about Canada, Mexico, France, or whatever foreign land some member of the audience might be visiting from. "Anyone come here to get a front-row view of the apocalypse?"

He turned toward Wu. "You seem like a distinguished gentleman. Where are you from?"

Willoughby was horrified by the attention.

Wu seemed game. "I am from the People's Republic of China."

A few people in the audience hissed and booed.

"Hey!" the MC upbraided them. "Don't be hissing and booing your fellow audience member—our guest from another country. This *gentleman* hasn't been shooting down our planes, sinking our ships, and aiming missiles at us. Or, I don't know, maybe he has." He turned to Wu. "Sir, do you have anything to do with this war that's going on?"

Wu stood, as if addressing a formal convention. "I can tell you with authority that there will be no more fighting," he proclaimed. "The war is over."

The audience seemed stunned, not quite sure if this was part of the act.

"Did you hear that?" the MC shouted. "See? You don't have to stay home and watch CNN or MSNBC to learn about the news. You can get your scoops right here at the Comedy Cellar. This gentleman says—*with authority*—the *war is over!* Let's give him a hand!"

Everyone applauded, some hollered "*woo-woo*," still not quite clear what was going on.

Willoughby looked out at the people in the audience and saw that one of them knew exactly what was going on. There was Natalie Gold, squeezing through the others at her table in the back of the club, then dashing up the stairs. She'd probably been hanging out at the Olive Tree, as Willoughby had suggested, then somehow followed him and the others down to the Cellar, as if she were part of the entourage, and taken a seat where she could find one. By this time, she would have known who Wu was, and, figuring that what he said was real, she would be heading upstairs to a seat in the cafe, taking the laptop out of her bag, logging on, and typing an exclusive flash headline. Willoughby would read it later that evening, and it was a barn burner:

SENIOR CHINESE OLIGARCH BREAKS NEWS AT N.Y. COMEDY CLUB: "THE WAR IS OVER"

Willoughby and his guests stayed to watch the entire seventy-five-minute show. All five of the comedians on the bill improvised a line or two about Wu's melodramatic proclamation when they came onstage.

The first comic turned it into his opener: "I was upstairs watching the news. Frightening stuff. They're warning us to be on the lookout for a Chinese man wearing a $5,000 suit who's escaped from a nearby insane asylum. He is armed and dangerous."

Wu laughed uproariously, permitting the others at his table to laugh too.

At the end of the show, while the rest of the audience paid their bills and filed out the front door onto the sidewalk, Willoughby and his associates, still mirthful, were led up the back steps to the Olive Tree.

"That was wonderful!" Wu exclaimed, all smiles.

"The joke about waking up German in Stuttgart—that was hilarious!" Rostov chimed in.

Willoughby stared wide-eyed at Douglass, shaking his head, dazed by the whole improbable experience.

As they came into the café, Dworman eagerly approached them, and Willoughby made introductions.

"Welcome to the club," Dworman said. "I hope you had a good time."

"We made history up in your stepmother's apartment," Wu said, shaking Dworman's hand, then leaned in to whisper something in his ear.

"I can't speak for her paintings, but she drew all of these sketches." Dworman pointed to the dozens of artworks that lined the Olive Tree's walls. "Please, take any one of them, as a memento."

"Thank you," Wu said. "I am very moved."

By this time, the Olive Tree was filling up with diners, and the nervous security teams—Chinese, Russian, and American—rushed the emissaries out of the café and into their respective limos, which were parked just outside. Willoughby stayed behind. He looked around for Natalie Gold and saw her at the bar, talking on her cell phone. She looked over at him, smiled, and waved.

He turned to Dworman, thanked him profusely, asked him to keep quiet about the meeting, at least for the next twenty-four hours, and promised to come back soon.

Gold walked over.

Willoughby took her hand and introduced her to Dworman. "This is the world's greatest defense reporter."

"I know," Dworman replied. "She told me all about herself. That's why I let her follow you down to the Cellar."

Willoughby and Gold hailed a taxi and made it to Penn Station's Moynihan Train Hall just in time to catch the last Acela to Washington DC. They sat together in the first-class car, which was almost empty, maybe because few first-class passengers took the train so late at night, maybe because, not yet knowing the war was over, few passengers of any sort were keen to journey to ground zero.

Gold told Willoughby that she'd been on the phone with the editor of the *Washington Post*, where she once worked. She'd been thinking all week that it might be a good time to shut down her elite subscription newsletter and return to writing for the mass public again. The ups and downs of world politics were too important to keep her scoops bundled up for insiders. The move would mean a drastic pay cut, but she didn't need more money. *The Gold Mine* had made her a small fortune, which shrewd investments had swelled to a medium-sized fortune. She'd sent the *Post*'s editor her "War Is Over" scoop and offered to write, as her debut feature, a much longer piece that traced the full inside story of the war and the peace. She asked only that, as a staff reporter, she be given carte blanche to carve out her own beat and pursue her own stories. The editor, who'd been following *The Gold Mine*, eagerly agreed.

For nearly the rest of the trip home, Willoughby recounted the events of the past week from his vantage point, then described the strange meeting in the top-floor apartment above the Comedy Cellar. He spoke on background, meaning he wasn't to be identified as a source. He insisted that none of the participants' names be mentioned, including his.

After some hesitation, he told her about Wu's monologue on the tragic paradox of deterrence and the senior politicians' pretense that they didn't hear it, so she could fully appreciate the stakes of what had just happened. But he urged her, practically begged her, not to report that part of the story.

Gold promised to be discreet. "As I once told you, I don't reveal my sources, and I don't blow ongoing intelligence operations. I also don't write anything that increases the chances of World War III."

They arrived at Washington's Union Station around midnight and took a taxi to Willoughby's apartment. They sat in silence, mulling what their ride's destination meant for what was likely to happen next.

Meanwhile, they were both famished. Their first moves after entering his apartment were toward the kitchen. Willoughby took out a baguette that he'd bought the night before, a few wraps of cheese, a roll of Italian salami, and a bottle of Pinot Noir, which he opened and poured into two wide-rimmed glasses.

They ate and drank as if they'd been fasting for days.

"I have to ask you something," Willoughby said, breaking the silence. "When we had our first lunch, not that long ago, how did you know that I was into Harold Feinstein photographs?"

Gold smiled. "From Danica, of course. We were classmates at Barnard, and we've stayed friends ever since. When you asked me to lunch, I called her to ask about you. She'd mentioned that the two of you had gone out a long time ago. She said that you and I might get along. 'He likes basketball, jazz, stand-up comedy, and urban street photography,' she told me, as if it were strange for anyone to have those enthusiasms."

She smiled again. "Yes, I already had the Feinstein book, and yes, I had the book of Auden poems, too. But that's what I'm telling you. I really did cherish them. Still do." She paused. "I was impressed that you didn't fall for my trap, that you didn't say '*You like Feinstein? I like Feinstein too!*' You knew what I was doing, and you weren't going to let me squeeze anything out of you so easily. I respected you for that." She paused again. "Still do."

Several more seconds lingered in silence. "Do you have an original vinyl pressing of Coltrane's *Ballads*?" she asked.

"I do," Willoughby replied, delighted at the question, though not so surprised—nothing about Natalie Gold was likely to surprise him at this point.

"Play it," she whispered, as she started unbuttoning her shirt.

CHAPTER 12

Willoughby woke up around 10:00 the next morning. It was Sunday. Exactly one week had passed since the fateful party at Wolf Mandelbaum's house. He sighed in relief that the nightmare was over, and he basked in the warm sensation of a blank page on his calendar. He saw a note from Gold next to his pillow. She'd been up for a few hours and had gone back to her place to do more reporting, then write her big story.

"See you tonight," the note ended, which soothed him back to sleep for another hour.

After waking up for good, he spent the rest of the day reading the paper, listening to music, and musing over his new status as a responsible global citizen, even if he'd attained it by sheer accident. He wondered whether he should feel any different—or *do* anything differently—from the way he had felt or acted before.

Gold texted him at 5:00. Her story had gone online a half hour earlier. She needed to stay at the office a little longer, to talk with her editor about upcoming stories and the whole arrangement of her new job. "How about sushi at 7:00," she proposed. He was fine with that. He was fine with anything.

He logged on to the *Washington Post*'s website, and there was her byline topped by a large-font headline, followed by an enormous piece—a comprehensive chronicle of how the war started, evolved, and ended, jammed with scoops, a head-spinning number of scoops, one after the other, only a few of which had come from Willoughby.

With steadily growing pleasure, he skimmed the competing news sites, which barely went beyond the president's announcement, not quite an hour earlier, of a ceasefire. He turned on the cable news channels, each for a few minutes. They were all quoting her story, with a particular focus on the comedy-club angle. He went back online and looked up the New York tabloids, which followed in kind, with their trademark snappy headlines:

OLIVE BRANCH AT THE OLIVE TREE

COMEDY CELLAR SUMMIT

MIRACLE ON MACDOUGAL STREET

None of the stories, including Gold's, mentioned Willoughby by name. Her story did refer to "the consultant" who popped up in the most unlikely segments of the tale. Careful readers might logically, though mistakenly, infer that the consultant in question was Wolf Mandelbaum, since a smaller *Post* story reported that he would be honored the next day with the Presidential Medal of Freedom "for his valiant work in advancing diplomacy over conflict."

The phone rang. It was Danica Bloom. "Had enough adventure for a while?"

"Well, I have some ideas on how to make peace in the Middle East," Willoughby replied with mock earnestness.

"Ha-ha, don't call us, we'll call you. Listen, have you heard that Wolf is getting a Presidential Medal of Freedom?"

"Yes, I just saw that. Don't worry. I won't go over and steal it."

"Actually, you should go over there and congratulate him," Bloom suggested rather firmly. "Really. And Chae-won wants to talk with you. She told me this expressly. She has something very specific to discuss."

Willoughby looked at his watch. He had a couple of free hours before meeting Gold for dinner. He might as well pay Mandelbaum a congratulatory visit. It was the least he could do, after his phone prank and all the tumult he'd caused.

"One more thing," Bloom said. "Your friend Greenway is in trouble with his masters at Fort Meade for helping us out on those phone tapes. I'm thinking of bringing him over to Langley. Do you know of any reason why I shouldn't?"

"No, no," he said casually. "No, he's great. Good move."

Hanging up, he made a note to call Greenway and urge him to check into some treatment center before taking the CIA polygraph test.

Willoughby grabbed a bottle of champagne (not his best bottle, but good enough), went downstairs, and hailed a cab to the Mandelbaums' house in Georgetown. He rang the bell.

Chae-won came to the door just a few seconds later. "Serge, so nice of you to stop by," she said in a quiet, almost meek voice. "Please, come in. Wolf will be so pleased to see you."

He handed her the champagne and expressed his congratulations: well-deserved encomium for a lifetime of fine work, and so forth.

"Yes, yes, yes," she said perfunctorily, almost coldly, setting the bottle down. She looked up at him with an intense glare. "Serge, I know that you were the one who made that phone call to the Chinese hardware store."

Willoughby tried to say something, but his vocal cords locked shut.

"I saw you going upstairs at the party that night," she went on, reciting a story that she'd probably been hankering to tell him for days now. "I didn't make anything of it at the time. I figured that the bathroom down here was occupied, so you went up there. But as Wolf and I sat in that dreadful FBI interrogation center, and as I learned what had happened and thought it over, it came to me—*you* must have been the one who did this."

Willoughby saw no point in denying it and started to mumble apologies, but she raised her palm, as if telling him to stop. "I know that you and Wolf haven't got along for many years. I suppose it dates back to the time when he asked you to come work for him, then tried to make his offer more appealing by getting his friends in the Pentagon to cancel their contracts with your company."

Willoughby had buried this incident in his subconscious for many years, but she was right: that betrayal probably was what set this whole thing off; it deepened his already-deep contempt for politics and his loathing of Wolf, culminating in the phone call that almost triggered World War III.

"That must have hurt," she went on, "and, though I don't think he ever said this to you, he told me a while later that he deeply regretted doing that. Between you and me, I think he was a bit jealous. You were the hot young consultant on the block. Wolf knew you were at least as good an analyst as he was, and a better mathematician. So, he snapped.

"But Serge, that is no excuse for you—all these years later, with all your subsequent success—to frame him on charges of espionage. That may not have been your intention—I know that you like playing games, maybe you just saw this as another game—but he almost *was* charged with espionage, and if he had been, I would have been charged as his accomplice."

"Chae-won, really—" Willoughby began, but she cut him off.

"Say no more. It's over and done. Forget about it. But there is one thing you can do. In fact, there's one thing you *must* do."

"Anything," he replied, maybe prematurely, but it didn't matter; she was clearly determined to force the issue, whatever it was.

"Wolf's mental capacity is not what it once was, and the past week's events—the arrest, the threats, the heart palpitations, and so forth—haven't helped. But he is very keen to get back in the action, and you are going to help him. I'm asking you to dissolve your corporation and to create a new firm with him. You can keep your office in DuPont Circle. You can keep your staff. You can still run the show. He wants a desk, four walls, and a door. He wants a piece of the equity for any contracts that he brings in. And he wants his name on the logo. He wants the new company to be called MMW— Mandelbaum, Molloy, & Willoughby. Yes, your friend Giles Molloy—our mutual friend—has agreed to come in on this, if just to keep the two of you from biting each other's heads off."

"Look, I don't know, Chae-won," Willoughby interrupted.

"What do you mean you don't know?" she said very sternly. "Here's the deal, Serge. Either you agree to this arrangement or I spread it all over town that you made that phone call, you framed Wolf for espionage, out of sheer spite. This town makes excuses for a lot of conniving behavior, but I don't think they'll make excuses for that. Your career, your reputation, will be finished."

Willoughby opened his mouth to speak, unsuccessfully.

"*And*," she went on, "I've been consulting my old law books in Wolf's library"—so those were *her* law books, Willoughby reflected—"and I'm pretty sure that you could be prosecuted for harassment, telephone fraud, willful interference with national security operations, maybe a few other felonies."

Willoughby paused. "Wolf's name has to be first on the masthead?" He realized as he said it that he was sounding awfully petty.

"It will be good for business. Have *you* ever won a Presidential Medal of Freedom? It comes with a lot of prestige and publicity."

Willoughby sighed. He'd been evading the near-certainty that he would have to pay a price for his perfidy. The universe practically demanded that he pay a price, and the prospect of sharing a suite of offices with Wolf Mandelbaum, odious as that might be, was a lot less odious than many alternatives.

"You've got a deal," he said, with some resignation.

"Good," Chae-won said, as if settling the matter. "Now go over and talk with him. He's in the kitchen."

Willoughby walked to the next room, still a bit uneasy.

"Hello, Serge!" Mandelbaum said, looking up from a bowl that he'd been stirring, genuinely excited. "Come over here. Have I ever shown you how to swirl the optimal amount of cheese on a stick of fondue?"

Willoughby rolled his eyes. Mandelbaum was such an asshole.

Then again, one lesson of the past week might be that it was time to junk the Janus Corporation and the hollow cynicism it embodied. Maybe with this new company, Willoughby, rather than playing both sides of the street, would take on just those projects, and reach just those conclusions, that he believed in—at least most of the time. If Mandelbaum was responsible, however unwittingly, for this renewed approach to life, business, and politics, then maybe even assholes can serve a purpose.

THE END

Fred Kaplan

ACKNOWLEDGEMENTS

Many thanks to Nell Minow of Miniver Press, for taking this on; Nell Scovell, for making introductions; Mira Singer, for sharp copyediting; Rachael Adams, for the very cool cover; Chris & Oriole Mullen, for their encouragement and for bringing Rachael onboard; Peter Pringle, for longstanding wise words; my agent, Rafe Sagalyn; and my family—Brooke Gladstone, Maxine Kaplan, and Sophie Kaplan—for their usual moral support and, this time, shrewd literary counsel as well.

ABOUT THE AUTHOR

FRED KAPLAN is *Slate*'s War Stories columnist and the author of six nonfiction books, including *The Insurgents: David Petraeus and the Plot to Change the American Way of War*, which was a New York Times Bestseller and a Pulitzer Prize Finalist. Others include *The Bomb*, *Dark Territory*, *1959*, *Daydream Believers*, and *The Wizards of Armageddon*. He has written for the *New York Times*, *Washington Post*, *The New Yorker*, and the *New York Review of Books*, among many publications, and also reviews jazz records for *Tracking Angle*. Long ago, he was a reporter for the *Boston Globe*, based in Washington, Moscow, and New York, and, during that time was a lead member of the team that won a Pulitzer Prize for a special Sunday magazine on the nuclear arms race. Kaplan has been awarded fellowships with the Council on Foreign Relations, New America, the American Academy in Berlin, and the London School of Economics. He graduated from Oberlin College and, like the novel's hero, earned a Ph.D. in political science from M.I.T., then briefly worked as a defense-policy adviser in the US House of Representatives. (Unlike the hero, he has never been a consultant.) He lives in Brooklyn with his wife, Brooke Gladstone.

For more information: http://fredkaplan.info

Made in the USA
Coppell, TX
20 January 2025

44659911R00098